SCARS

by

DAMON MAHER

ZEUS

SCARS
Copyright © Damon Maher 2005

First published in 2005 by
Zeus publications
http://www.zeus-publications.com
P.O. Box 2554
Burleigh MDC. Qld. 4220
Australia

ISBN: 1-9210-0546-7

This is a work of fiction and any resemblance to persons living or dead is purely coincidental.

About the author

Damon Maher was born in the United Kingdom in 1973. He studied English Literature at Brunel University in West London before migrating to Australia in 2000. He teaches English (and soccer) at Kinross College in Perth's northern suburbs. Damon lives with his wife and two sons. 'Scars' is his first novel.

Dedication

For Samuel and Liam

Acknowledgements

Huge thanks to Tanya for her loving support and editing expertise. To Martin for his wonderful cover design. To Mum and Dad for always being there. To Josh for his work with the website (www.damonmaher.com) and to everyone at Zeus for teeing up this opportunity for me.

Scar /ska:/ **1** a permanent mark on the skin left after the healing of a wound. **2** the lasting effect of grief etc. on a person's character or disposition. **3** a mark left by damage.

Concise Oxford Dictionary

1
Sunday (the morning after): 7:32 am

I was stuck between the past and the future. Somewhere between madly in love and young, free and single. Between the nervous excitement of a new career and that stage at work where you're regarded as part of the fixtures and start getting precious over your coffee mug. I was living like an adult in the week and a teenager at the weekend. And, at that very moment in time, I was somewhere between asleep and awake, waiting for one hell of a hangover to kick in.

Sundays. Start off happy, end up sad, whatever happens in between. I lie in, drink tea, go down the shop, read the papers, eat a cholesterol sandwich, then venture back to the pub to watch the football and prove to myself I *can* enjoy a couple of drinks without it turning into something blurry and nauseous. Then it's all over, no sooner am I toasting the endless possibility of two whole days off than I'm grunting a sour hello at the start of another week.

The passion for the job has ebbed away, seeping silently like an old inner tube. I used to love teaching. The search for the perfect lesson, the behaviour management strategies, extending the brainiacs, holding on tight to the kids at risk, the ones with the goldfish attention spans. It used to be a challenge, until I found my comfort zone. I still like it, the holidays, the friends I've made, the fact I finish at four in the afternoon. I even like the kids, some of them, the ones who would be my friends, my fancies, if I were their age. The ones who don't expect too much of me, they're my favourites. I still put the effort in, into making myself look like I care; like staying late to surf the net at my desk so as to appear like I'm not a clock watcher, even though I'm probably the most adept clock watcher in the entire school, including the kids. I'm good at playing the system, at giving the students most of what they need, all with an economy of effort that makes me proud of myself. That's my challenge now. And I succeed, every day.

I'm a nice teacher, too. The kids like me, probably because my expectations of them have been duly dropped by my own apathy. I'm no hypocrite, I don't expect more than I'm willing to give. That wouldn't be fair. And I'm a role model of sorts, straddling the fence between limited success and obvious failure, showcasing the subtle nuances of work avoidance, promoting the virtues of just doing enough. I'm certainly not as mean, uptight or downright ugly as the teachers of my day. I don't have an innate hatred of adolescents, a penchant for vulgar ties or an ability to cultivate dandruff the size and consistency of frosted cornflakes. They were just there to baby-sit, to give our parents a break, to fill our young heads with useless tosh and to live out their Nazi-fuelled fantasies whilst remaining this side of the law. I'm not like that, which is progress of sorts.

They were my incentive. Those bastards. Their ineptitude triggered my desire to teach. No, hang on a minute, that's not entirely true. That would be my stock answer if questioned by a student, a parent, a senior member of staff or a member of staff of equal standing whom I didn't trust as far as I could throw. The real reasons for my entry into education were thus: I'd run out of time, inclination, ideas and money. Teaching was a last resort.

It comes down to two things, really. First, I hate getting up, and second, I love days off. No offence to working or anything but if it thinks it can compete with time off then it's got another think coming. Maybe if you're a footballer or a rock star or something, but then you're not really working are you? You're just doing exactly what you want, and getting paid loads for it.

This particular Sunday seemed lovely. Through half open eyes I could see a single shaft of dusty sunlight pierce the gap between my curtains. I toyed with the air's pleasant chill, flirting playfully before coiling back into my duvet. And, for one fleeting moment, before my brain was in gear, during that fraction of a second that contains a million thoughts, this particular Sunday *was* lovely. And I told myself that after a short bout of secondary sleep, I'll get up. I'll throw on a friendly tracksuit and wander outside, with Donnie and Connor, my two best friends and long-term flatmates. Together we'll cluster, shiver and giggle, like kids, not a care in the world, dawdling to the corner shop for Sunday supplies: ciggies, papers, bacon, eggs, coke, multipack of crisps; an age-old assemblage that helps soften the dull thump of a hangover.

And, despite cutting a bedraggled and gormless figure, I'd be happy; a bemused grin plastered on my pale, damp face. I'll nod, release an incoherent mumble in the vague direction of Mr Patel and he'll smile back, eye me up and down and take solace in the fact his religion frowns upon the consumption of alcohol. We'll then itch our collective scalp, pick up a basket and bumble about in search of comfort food.

Mr Patel, who owns and runs the store, is always pleased to see us on a Sunday morning. Indeed, if he were a cartoon character there would be dollar signs where his eyes should be. For we are in a certain state of mind, one of frivolity and confusion. We are slaves to the hangover. When we stumble into his store, Mr P gets both comedic entertainment and the opportunity to offload half his shop. We have no concept of monetary value. Why would we? We've just spent a small fortune on a night we can hardly remember.

But sadly that moment soon slides.

My mind clicks into gear. The horrific events of last night steal in. My eyes burst open; I spring out of bed, my head spinning with the realization that this particular Sunday isn't lovely. It isn't lovely at all. Or at least it couldn't be lovely anymore. I rub my eyes until tiny stars flicker in the air in front of me, then stumble across the hallway to bang my palm on Donnie's door. But he's already up. He's showered, dressed and sitting silently in the kitchen.

Donnie looks up and smiles weakly.

'Ready?' I ask.

'Let's go, Sam,' he replies.

His facial expression is one of a man suffering a hangover, all wayward fringe and baggy-eyed. Normally I'd find this funny. But today isn't normal and I don't feel much like laughing. Our hangover isn't about drinking too much. How I wish that it were. Five minutes later we're sitting in Donnie's car, shuffling uncomfortably, no music, no talking, no sign of life. I catch my reflection in the wing mirror but it doesn't look like me. My face looks old and loose; a sickly shade of grey save for the pale blue bruising that slowly melts into my eyes.

The doors slam, our belts click in and the engine groans angrily into gear. As we reverse the tyres spin hard, kicking up gravel and spitting it into the side of the car. I peer down the pathway in search of dry blood or skin or teeth or any other evidence of last night's fight. I can't see anything, save for the remnants of someone's Saturday night supper: brownish salad bits and damp, crumpled paper, in amongst the grey gravel. I don't know where the proof would be anyway; it all looks so different in the daylight.

We move onto the road and on towards the lights. We are heading straight for the local hospital.

2
Sunday: 7:58am

My thoughts soon drift towards Nicole, like tired old homing pigeons, out of habit, unwilling and unable to break the cycle. Again, my time is being monopolised by an ex-girlfriend who, by all accounts, is now ensconced in a new relationship, with a new man. Probably a *New Man*. All empathy, sympathy and aroma-fucking-therapy. Meanwhile, a bevy of marauding grey cloud has ambushed the sickly weak sunshine that greeted me first thing. Drops of rain have developed into a heavy downpour, mimicking my general malaise.

After a stuttering start we stop at the lights. My eyes are drawn to a playground on my left. There are two children there, playing together, twins maybe, with their father. His day for access. I remember it well; I was much older than them. They're enjoying their run-around, between breakfast at McDonald's and the matinee movie. They scamper about, sliding, shouting, cradled by their own naivety. I compare badly today. I am slouching, aching, trying desperately to put aside the mental picture of my best friend being beaten unconscious, his head bouncing off the ground, breaking like an egg.

The lights remain a blurry, watery red. The windscreen wipers slide and squeak and the rain drums hard against the window. We inch slowly, clattering through a wall of water that builds steadily by the roadside, like a mote between childhood innocence and me. The sense of separation is unbearable. Suddenly there's an unwelcome tear making its awkward journey down the side of my face. The sensation is excruciating. It tickles intensely, running over every contour and groove that guards my eye before falling onto the back of my hand, magnifying the lines of age and growth. Suddenly I *feel* old, which is infinitely worse than just looking it. I tried hard to retrieve those feelings of youth, of innocence, but there was nothing there. They'd meandered away, like the purity of a sleeping child. Adults don't look the same when they're asleep. We look drained, half-dead, like we've just hit a wall and fallen into bed.

Something had to give. My train of thought had derailed, leaving me reeling at the complexity of my feelings. My thought pattern, in contrast, had proven alarmingly simple …

It's raining. I feel grumpy when it rains. Look at all those kiddies. Bless 'em. They look happy. I don't think I'm very happy. I used to be happy. I feel happy when it's sunny. It was sunny in Australia. I was in Australia with Nicole. Nicole is not my girlfriend anymore. I think I'm going to cry in the car …

The car is awash with mist and stale air. I open the window, tiny bullets of rain fire in, but the air is good, refreshingly cold on my damp forehead. I wipe my eye, sniff sharply and hope Donnie hasn't seen my momentary lapse. He hasn't. He's too busy wondering about what he's going to say to Connor.

Rather him than me, I think.

Clearly I'm struggling to control my emotions. It isn't surprising. After all, they lay dormant for so much of my life, getting a brief airing during my first *bona fide* relationship at school with the brazen Abby North; a schoolyard, hometown romance of minimal emotional substance that petered out upon the news that Abby was to answer her calling and become a nurse.

Her insistence on being a real adult was in direct contrast to my sideways thrust into the wishy-washy world of English literature, and so we went our separate ways, with the vast majority of my emotional bullion still firmly stuck in the vault. And there it remained until Nicole discovered the code, dusted it down and teased it all out. And now I've been left alone with it, this bar of hardened emotional residue; and I'm teetering under its weight, staring hard without recognizing one miserly nugget.

It's kind of like watching football on the TV without having full control of the remote. This wouldn't be so bad if either Connor or Donnie were in charge of it. I could sit in relative calm knowing that although the technical expertise - volume control and half-time channel hopping duties - were in the hands of another, there would be no outrageous button-flicking whilst the game was in progress. But to have your ex-girlfriend in charge of your feelings, well, that's tantamount to handing over the remote control on a silver platter to my belligerent, flatulent, sport-hating grandmother. You've no idea what's going to happen; you just know it's going to be unpleasant.

The virtuoso of my heartstrings quit playing our song a while back now. Most of the time I'm fine. But there doesn't seem an awful lot I can do when I'm not fine. No control. I have incontinence of the heart. At first I put my personal turmoil down to emotional amputation, like losing a limb and expecting it to be there. Donnie said it was like a virus that needed to work its way through my system. He suggested a trip to Amsterdam and a knuckle sandwich for the new guy. Connor said I should call her, he reckoned we had *unfinished business*. I wasn't sure what to do. I *was* sure of one thing though: I wasn't ready for her to move on. I resented the notion of being an ever-decreasing memory, my life diluted to insignificance, nothing but a benchmark for someone else to improve upon.

'Do you think he hates me?'

It was Donnie.

'What?'

'Is Connor going to be pissed off with me?'

'Course he won't, Don.'

'It's my fault he's in there.'

'No it's not. And Connor knows that.'

'If I'd stayed well out of it, kept my big mouth shut, then Connor wouldn't be in hospital right now. There would never have been that fight and our mate wouldn't have been beaten up by a bunch of psychopathic gangsters.'

Donnie's hands were gripping tight on the wheel. His skin, normally dark and handsome, was stretched and pale, with reddened grazing on his knuckles. He was on the edge. I'd never seen him so prickly and fretful. And the truth is, there was a part of me - some shady, shameful little hole - that was enjoying it. If my prim and steely English reserve was being jarred by the events of last night then I didn't see why his *laissez-faire* Aussie cool should make it through unscathed.

Still, he was my friend, and he needed support. So I plumped for the knee-jerk humour option.

'Look Don, Connor will probably thank you. Think about it. There's free grub in there for the tight-arse, a bed with *clean* sheets and loads of lovely nurses. He'll have a couple of bed baths and the phone number of some big-breasted Matron by the time we arrive.'

Donnie looked unconvinced.

I felt unconvincing.

And I think I probably sounded it too.

As we approached the car park, I too became anxious. My head was a mess. I have two best mates; one was in hospital and the other one blamed himself, probably rightly so. Add to that those bad doses of regret about my ex-girlfriend, a foggy hangover that refused to clear and a nose that appeared to be broken, and you're starting to get the picture.

I looked up at the sky, searching for a patch of blue, hoping things would somehow get better. But the brightness was behind us.

All I could see was gunmetal grey.

How the hell did this all happen?

3
Saturday night (the night before): 7:24pm

Rod Stewart once said to me 'you can beat an egg but you can't beat a Saturday night'. Wise words indeed, and they've remained etched on my heart ever since, undiluted by the fact he said them to fifteen thousand other fans at the same time.

Saturday nights *are* great. Friday nights are good but Saturday nights are great. Friday nights have the potential to be great but more often than not there's too many obstacles: tiredness, time restrictions, lack of proper mates, abundance of useless work colleagues, you're too far from home, still got your bag, you just want to eat, there's good TV on, and you're wary of not ruining your whole Saturday with a hangover gained from a night that simply wasn't worth it. Your best bet with Friday night is one of those spontaneous sessions where everyone's suddenly in the right mood.

Such nights seldom come however and Saturday night remains the undisputed champion of the week. And on this particular Saturday night we decided to go for a few beers down our local pub. The Fox and Hounds sits cosily by the Thames and, more importantly, just minutes from our flat. Over the last

11

few years we've managed to graduate to the prestigious rank of regulars; no mean feat considering our first few visits were met with a stifled hush and more than the odd cold stare. Darts hovered mid-throw, the jukebox jolted to a conspicuous standstill as we entered under the somewhat optimistic 'welcome' sign. There were plenty of other pubs within walking distance, but this was the nearest, it was on our street, therefore was our local, even if it's regular patrons didn't share our reasoning. And potentially it had a great atmosphere, if you could just penetrate that inner-circle.

So we sat, drank and waited for positive eye contact. It got a bit hairy on occasion, especially when Donnie inadvertently upset the cueing arm of 'Misery' Morris when he was on the verge of beating his archrival Darren 'Monkey' Taylor ('Monkey' as in *grease* – he's a dodgy mechanic whose stuttering business is subsidised by the selling of 'adult' films to 'certain' customers from the back of his garage). Misery Morris is an ex-fairground boxer with a weakness for soccer hooliganism and, as a general rule, his arm's the wrong one to nudge. However, this incident proved the icebreaker. We bought a generous round by way of apology and spent the remainder of the evening getting acquainted with the regulars. It turned out I taught some of their kids. They wanted honest appraisals on how good their boys were at football and whether or not their daughters had unsavoury reputations. It was clearly the communal dream to produce either an international soccer star or a girl who kept her knickers on. They'd also heard of Donnie's old man, Bob Rossi, a living legend on this patch, his name etched in London folklore. This in spite of the fact he'd been living in

Australia for the past twenty-five years. It was Donnie's surname that cut the ribbon. Now Donnie was reaping the rewards, though he felt a little uncomfortable about it.

This all occurred a fair few years back. We're now at the stage where *we* treat newcomers with an unhealthy mix of paranoia, rudeness and fear. According to Large Barry, our landlord, you're better off assuming everyone you don't know is either a plain-clothes detective or the taxman. It's a piece of advice I'm loath to take on board, yet with the relentless passing of time and the incessant will of human nature I seem to be fighting a losing battle against becoming a self-contained, slightly standoffish, middle-aged bloke. It's the antithesis of a plaque that sits serenely on my grandmother's mantelpiece: *There are no such things as strangers, only friends we haven't met yet*. If The Fox and Hounds had a plaque - which is unlikely, it hasn't even got a menu, just a dusty old chalkboard and an alcoholic chef with a reasonably good memory - it would probably read: *Everyone is a stranger, until you're a local*. Which is okay, because we're all locals now.

Large Barry can be quite astute at times. He can also be a grumpy fat bastard but you take the rough with the smooth when he's the one in charge of the lager. The reason we call him 'Large' Barry has nothing to do with either the contents of his underpants or the size of his bank balance - he hasn't had a proper look at either of those for some years now. It's because of his sizeable frame. It would probably be more apt if he were nicknamed Fat Barry, Obese Barry, Double D-cup Barry or One-fried-egg-sandwich-away-from-your-

13

third-coronary Barry. But, again, seeing as he's the bloke who pulls the pints, we refer to him fondly as 'Large'. It's a more fluid term and could, perhaps, refer to an obsession with bodybuilding - as long as you'd never met him of course.

London can be an unyielding city, hard work if you're feeling weak, downright unhealthy for the soul if you're feeling lonely. It's full of tourists getting cosy highs on history. It's quick and it works. And it works for us to have a place that wouldn't interest your average tourist. As a group we've always tried hard to maintain an acceptable level of immaturity and our local pub is one of the few places we know that positively encourages us to do so. Toilet humour is expected and sport is treated like religion. There's no dress code, kids' menu or playground, and meals come without garnish. But when you do order a pub lunch you get a damn good plateful. And that plateful, like the pub itself, fills a gap. No one's going to rip you off in there - not if they know you. Half of them may look like they'd happily rip you apart but their collective bark is worse than their bite. I think it was Connor who recently, proudly, referred to himself as a 'twenty-six-year-old boy'. Like cheap wine, we are maturing badly. We can just about cope with keeping our jobs and putting the bins out on a Tuesday. Anything more would be dangerous.

Student life didn't help much. It hardly prepared us for the world outside the campus walls. We just built up a hefty debt and an impressive resistance to alcohol. Then, because we hung around long enough, they handed us a degree at the graduation ceremony. So we went out to celebrate. By getting drunk, naturally. That next hangover proved the worst, however; the headache of real life; with real people, real tiredness. It's quite a shock - horrific really. Especially when you start spouting hackneyed truisms like *early to bed, early to rise* and *another day, another dollar*. There's the train full of suits, weekends full of ironing; I used to wonder how real people - grown-ups and non-students - managed to fit in a full-time job. Now I know. You just have to forget about everything else.

There were plenty of downsides to student life too. Like being skint and living in a pigsty with fellow dung beetle hybrids. There was always a damp mattress in the garden, green stuff in the fridge and cheap toilet roll in the bog, the stuff that doubled up as tracing paper. And then there was the milk. The sour, neglected milk. It was a long time before I could physically pour the stuff on cereal again. I still smell the top. Just in case. You know, what with the lumps and that.

If all the wives of the hot-shot lawyers, the respected physicians and the high-flying executives knew what their husbands had got up to, how they'd existed at university, there'd be mayhem in the middle classes, chaos in the country-style kitchens throughout the land. Wine racks would roll and fondue sets would fly if the homemakers and housewives knew the real truth of the men behind the broadsheets, before the sensible footwear and the gardening shows.

It was just another Saturday night. Or so we thought. By the end of it Connor was in hospital and Donnie and I were in shock. Four hours before we entered the emergency ward we strolled into the Fox and Hounds, blissfully unaware of how the night was to unfold.

15

First the good news: we were starting the night together. It's always advisable to begin on an equal footing as far as alcohol's concerned. If the person you're meeting is significantly more inebriated than you, it can be awkward, like looking into a window to the future. Three hours down the line and that sad bastard is you. All the slurring, the spitting, the unnecessary hugs, the smelly burps, the total disregard for personal space and the incessant bullshit; that's you, that is.

So often these days our meetings are staggered. It's got so complicated, messy even. There's other faces, other bars, different times, different friends; workmates and rugby chums, late shifts and early starts. I couldn't remember the last time we'd actually walked into the Fox on a Saturday night together.

But, as we did, so Connor went and ruined it, his Irish eyes lighting up at an opportunity to embarrass me. From the moment I first clapped eyes on him, over fifteen years ago - his freckle-faced features full of untold mischief - he's been out to get me. It's his *raison d'etre*. When you're eleven it's a good thing. Any kid who can guarantee an endless supply of trouble is well worth sticking close to. But these days it's harder to deal with.

We all noticed the barmaid, partly because she was new, mainly because she was hot. But before any of us had the chance to become acquainted, Connor started playing up. He pretended to be gay. Not only did he pretend to be gay, he pretended I was his boyfriend, mincing up to the bar like Elton John on acid. He grabbed me by the arm and, in the most effeminate voice he could muster, squealed toward the new barmaid.

'Hi sweetie, love the nails. Eyes off this one though, he's spoken for. We bat for the other team, if you catch my drift. You should see this one bowl me off a good length; he can't half swing a ball, let me tell you.'

'Sorry?'

She wore the single most bemused look I'd ever seen. No doubt I wore the second. You'd think I'd have gotten used to all this by now but being Connor's best friend is a bit like going to the dentist. No matter how often you see them you never get used to it; because somewhere along the line it's going to get painful. Donnie, on the other hand, loved every second. His immeasurable self-assurance allows him to enjoy Connor's antics like a paying spectator, thus avoiding any fallout. It's like he's got an embarrassment deflector shield, one that points directly at me. Connor was relentless. His wrist was limp, his lips were pursed and his dander was undeniably up. She had no chance. And I had even less.

'I'm new here,' she said.

And that wasn't helping either. Quite the opposite, it was fuelling him, probably the very reason he'd piped up in the first place. Now I'm no homophobe. I have a brother who is gay. But let's be honest, you don't want someone that good looking thinking you sit on the other side of the church, do you? And nor did I want Connor getting the better of me, not here, not in my local, not again. Enough was enough. I jumped in with the first pathetic one-liner/poor excuse I could think of.

'Don't mind our friend here, he's on day release from the local loony bin and needs a drink so he can take his medication.'

It was neither original nor funny but, as it turned out, eminently believable. We hadn't reckoned on the gullibility of the new barmaid. She bought every word. She tipped her head to one side, unleashed a patronizing *aaahhh*, patted Connor's hand and asked if he wanted lager or bitter.

So we ordered our drinks and looked for somewhere to sit.

'You really are a complete tit, aren't you Connor?' I couldn't let it lie. I tried to reprimand Connor. But friends are notoriously hard to tell off. They just don't take you seriously.

'Don't be such a bitch,' he replied, refusing to abandon his character.

Meanwhile Donnie was chatting up the new barmaid, his *raison d'etre*. Every so often she'd giggle, and squeeze his arm. At one point I saw him lean over the bar and whisper in her ear. She roared with laughter, the whole pub hearing the howl in her retort, 'Donnie, you cheeky bugger.'

He finally joined us, twenty minutes later, trying to stem the imminent ridicule by bearing gifts. He was carrying a tray so packed with booze and snacks that a couple of packets of salted peanuts fell in my lap on impact. He wanted to avoid being set upon. He didn't want to be called a ladies' man, someone who chased skirt at the expense of quality time with his so-called friends. But as far as I was concerned he wasn't squirming off the hook that easily. Such powers are rendered useless on men. I didn't know why it bothered me so much. It never had done before, not to this extent anyway. But it did now.

Me: 'You just can't help yourself, can you? When are you going to learn that shallow relationships are a meaningless waste of time?'

Donnie: 'I was just being friendly. The chick's new; I was simply offering her a warm welcome. It's called *being polite*. No need to crack the shits, Sam.'

Connor: 'I bet that's not the only warm thing you were offering her, eh Donnie boy? Tell you what though pal, you can chat up the Queen bloody Mother if it means you get in a quality round like this afterwards. Lovely-jubbly.'

So there I was, on the verge of disclosing what I saw as a genuine psychological flaw in Donnie's character, and all Connor could do was undermine me. They were clearly ganging up. Then, just as I was about to unleash a verbal tirade on the pair of them, one that may well have ensued in me storming out the pub like a petulant child, Connor shut me up. And he did so because he knows me. He knows me very well. He not only knew that something was up, he also knew what it was, even before I did.

'So Sam,' he barked, staring straight at me, 'would you care to explain exactly what, or *who,* has rattled your cage?'

It was a rhetorical question. Or at least I turned it into one by refusing to answer it. Instead I acknowledged his perspicacity by cracking half a smile. Then I sighed. It was a long, slow release and I felt better for it. It wasn't Donnie who had rattled my cage, nor was it Connor. It was Nicole.

I really should have apologised, explained. But, in truth, there was more chance of me pulling out my manhood, slapping it on the table and asking the boys to take peanut pot shots at it than there was of me using this forum as a makeshift therapy session. That comes from my father. He was no good at owning up, coughing up or facing up either. I don't know if this was due to stubbornness, pride or an innate inability to own responsibility, I just know I could feel it too, growing inside of me. I also knew that, sooner or later, Connor would haul up the subject of Nicole for real. He was just waiting for me to slip into a calmer state of mind, one less inhibited by pent-up frustration, brought on by booze, one that would see me in a more candid state. He'd be waiting a long time, I thought. But he waited nevertheless. And as he waited I got more loaded; more wired on booze, nicotine and suppressed emotion.

In the meantime we talked about one-night stands. Connor was fascinated with Donnie's numbers and stories, he always was. We both were. I had little in terms of return fire, however. It annoyed me that Donnie refused to disclose his all-time favourite one-night stand. After all, it was he who'd picked the topic in the first place. The least he could do was let us live vicariously through him for a moment. Yet he kept us dangling, offering instead a half-interesting story about a near miss with a Singapore lady-boy. I don't know why he was being so coy; it wasn't his usual style, which is more kiss-and-tell than dignified silence.

Eventually we get there. To the whole Nicole thing. And I did my usual trick, of locking the vault and closing down the shutters.

Donnie: 'Do you still love her?'

Me: *(of course I do)* 'I'm not sure. Yes and no.'

Connor: 'What do you mean? You either do or you don't. It's like being half pregnant. You either are or you're not.'

Me: *(I love her. I love her. I fucking love her and you know it.)* 'I'm not sure whether I'm still *in* love with her.'

Donnie: 'Do you want her back?'

Me: *(yes)* 'I don't know, to be honest.'

Connor: 'Would you take her back?'

Me: *(yes, tomorrow)* 'I'd have to have a good, long think about it. A lot's happened and it would take time.'

Donnie: 'Would it ever be the same? You know, after everything that's happened?'

Me: *(I could cope. We'd make it work)* 'I don't know if I could cope. I'm not sure we could make it work.'

I churned out glib retort after glib retort, bleating on about a man's pride, fish in the sea, pastures new, onwards and upwards, my freedom, my space, blah, blah, blah. Connor assured me that 'denial's not a river in Egypt'. Donnie added that 'he who hesitates masturbates'. But, in spite of the profundity of their advice, I was feeling far too sorry for myself to take any notice, too busy convincing myself that Nicole was deeply in love. Again. I'd already assumed the two of them lived in each other's pockets, spending half their time in bed, popping up for air every couple of days to attend a free poetry recital in the park or an obscure European Film festival at the community centre.

'Yes, I can see it now,' I said, starting to feel a bit tipsy and twitchy. 'He's probably driving her around in his 2CV as we speak, burning joss sticks on the dashboard, playing his favourite homemade compilation tape of whiny student tosh.'

I was starting to lose it.

'And, what's more, what really irks the living crap out of me, is that he's probably rolling her fat joints and forcing gallons of cheap claret down her neck in a callous attempt to get her in the sack.'

Going, going.

'This sad little arsehole is taking advantage of my girlfriend, sorry, my *ex*-girlfriend, at an incredibly vulnerable time in her life.'

Gone.

I think I was almost shouting at the end. One of those pathetic, quivery shouts that live on the edge of tears. The pregnant pause that followed was practically in labour by the time someone else spoke. I can't remember who it was. I was too busy drinking.

His name is Toby. The new boyfriend. I didn't like acknowledging the fact he had a real name, or a real personality, or a real cock for that matter. I hated a man I'd never even met. On the occasion Connor had spotted them in town together, Toby was apparently wearing open-toe sandals and a Hawaiian shirt. And I hated him for that too. What's more, I now hated *anyone* who wore comfortable summer footwear with little regard for fashion or silly loud shirts that were clearly an attempt at bolstering a dull and lifeless personality. According to Nicole's brother, he was a nice enough chap who treated her well at a vulnerable time in her life. But who cares about that? He was seeing a damn sight more of Nicole than I was, and I definitely hated him for that.

We eventually put my outburst behind us and I successfully diverted the conversation in Donnie's direction. He was currently hanging on to single life by a thread, fervently denying having a girlfriend despite evidence to the contrary. He'd been seeing this girl called Amber Spears who, despite having the name of a porno star, was a quite stunning model from Putney and inexplicably besotted with Donnie. The feeling was mutual, but he refused to admit it, to either himself or us. Like me, Donnie was grappling new emotions that were seeing cold light for the first time. He didn't understand why, for example, he felt unexcited by the pursuit of the new barmaid. After all, she was both keen and gorgeous, usually *more* than enough for Donnie.

So, as is normally the case with such matters of national importance, Connor engineered a logical set of criteria in order to determine his status in the girlfriend / no girlfriend debate. And Donnie agreed to be grilled. The fool. The questions were rich and varied: how many dates, how much sex, phone call regularity, attendance at family gatherings, types of articles left at your place, etc. And at the end we totted up his score on a beer mat. It was an unqualified disaster.

On the relationship continuum Donnie was nearer to being married with a mortgage than single and on the market. The verdict shocked him so much he dashed straight for the bar and, in some pitiful, last ditch attempt to rescue a shattered ego, he tried it on with the barmaid. Yet his heart wasn't in it. Nor were his genitals. For the first time in twenty-six years of happy-go-lucky, the master of the trivial encounter was no more. It had been a wild and wonderful ride but now was over. So, dejected by his indifference to a chase he once revelled in, Donnie skulked back to our table. And, head cupped in hands, he accepted Connor's verdict and awaited his sentence.

Donnie was in love.

And he was truly devastated.

4
Saturday night: 11:34pm

The bells of doom rang their final, tragic chime and last orders came to a sad, undignified end. Large Barry, who'd been warned by the police about his after-hours drinking sessions, regretfully closed the pub on time. Tony the Greek threatened to chain himself to the fruit machine but Barry wouldn't budge.

Lock-ins are a privilege, not a right, and for once in his life our landlord was heeding the policeman's sage counsel. If his license were taken away it would be tragic. He'd be like the old New York Cop in the movies. The one who can't bear the thought of retirement. With his badge - or license - he *is* someone. Without it, he's just an overweight nobody with an unhealthy hankering for coffee and doughnuts. Or, in Barry's case: lager, cigarettes, fried food and soft porn. Without the pub, there'd be just three avenues of employment open to Barry: professional darts player, sumo wrestler or politician. But he's too untalented for the first, too unfit for the second and far too honest for the third.

So, seeing as a few extra pints were out of the question, we decided the best option for the remainder of the evening was a large doner kebab, the football highlights and a couple of chilled cans of lager back at our pad. The days of falling out of the pub on autopilot and heading straight for the nearest club are behind us. Only on special occasions do we venture out after midnight these days – birthdays, college reunions or those rare nights where you've had one too many and are incapable of acknowledging tiredness, inebriation or an inability to dance.

As we walked towards the front door of the pub I attempted to annoy Connor by suggesting his impression of an old queen was so good he may actually be one himself. He refused to bite. Instead, he farted loudly and blamed me. I felt the warm sensation of a full-blown blush and realized that the reddened cheeks on my face were only succeeding in incriminating the ones on my arse. My bum was on a hiding to nothing. He'd dropped one and charged me; a cheap trick, bereft of originality but capable of reaping plenty. The whole pub turned; men laughed and women scoffed. I felt like saying that if it's class and elegance you're after then why the hell are you drinking in here? But I didn't. I feel like saying a lot of things but never quite get round to them, especially in this place. I might be a regular but you never know who's with whom. Besides, there are a few women in here who'd happily beat me senseless without breaking sweat. One look at their tattooed necks and my balls shrivel up to half their normal size. Still, on this occasion I didn't deserve their daggers. Connor saw the pain in my eyes and went for the jugular. He scoffed in mock-bewilderment, unleashing an exaggerated tut, saying, 'Do you have to? How utterly childish, and in the presence of ladies, goodness me, you'll be lighting them next, you dirty bastard.'

We exit the rabble. I'm battle-weary, punch-drunk and short on ammunition. As we speak, hefty clouds of frozen breath swirl about us. It's markedly colder than earlier. My ears are raw; my bottom lip in spasm. I'm unleashing sharp, uncontrollable tremors and rattles so I light a cigarette, to fill the time, to see some glow of warmth. And, as we hunch our shoulders and sink our heads for the short stride home, I exhale its chilled smoke and curse the last cold snap of winter.

The air is biting, the darkness unnerving. I sense the wind through the treetops but I can see little save for the ghostly silhouettes of gates and the odd stipple of light on the river. There's the sporadic fizz of cars in the distance and the mishmash of our combined footsteps but beyond that there is silence. We head for the 'Kebab King' kebab shop, which is owned by Tony the Greek. However, Tony spends most of his time down the Fox and Hounds, leaving his sons to cut the meat from the revolving skewer. We buy our kebabs. As usual I ask for extra chilli sauce, because I'm drunk and therefore of the opinion that the hotter the food, the better the taste. Deep down I know I'll be scraping half of it off later.

When it's perishingly cold, when we're tired and hungry and when there's football to be watched, the rest of that short walk is like a red carpet. We feel lucky, minutes from bloke heaven. All that's required is a plate, a can, the remote control and a bar of the gas fire being put on. Ah sod it, we say, let's put two bars on; you only live once. Hang the expense.

Unfortunately this particular Saturday night was about to be severely disrupted. None of us were going to be watching or eating anything for a while. Waiting, yes, watching and eating, no. Twenty minutes later, the only thing I'm focused on is waiting for the ambulance to turn up. The only thing Donnie is focused on is stemming the steady flow of blood that falls into the gutter like rainwater, direct from Connor's head.

5
Saturday night: 11:58 pm

We were just minutes from home; minutes from the warmth and sanctity only your own place gives you. On the corner of our block of flats, clustered in the doorway, was a group of people, standing and talking. We had to pass them to get to the door that leads to our flat. My hand was deep in my pocket, rummaging for my keys. There were six men and one woman. The closer we got, the more menacing it felt. The mood was thick, a dim and daunting air hung about them. The woman was visibly upset, scared. She was shaking her head, whimpering, crying. Suddenly, simultaneously, we stopped, just metres from them. They turned towards us; I could see one of them had his hand wrapped around the girl's throat. He didn't relinquish the grip upon seeing us. If anything, he tightened it.

For a moment everyone stared, each computing his next move. I felt sick, my stomach a cauldron of fusty grog and apprehension. We'd unknowingly disturbed something, and now we were a factor; from strangers to bystanders to participants in ten seconds flat.

The men were all dressed in black or dark clothing; collars obscured parts of faces, and what was left was awesome, ugly. These weren't simply boys on the town, looking for a ruck at chucking-out time, in between last orders and the Curry House. They were proper trouble, the kind of people you were meant to avoid. But we were standing beside them. Toe to toe.

We said nothing and did nothing, and if it wasn't for the fact that in amongst this wall of black clothing and hideous flesh stood a petrified girl, sobbing and shaking, we'd have walked straight past them and out of trouble, united by mutual, unspoken desire for a healthier space. One of them turned, slowly lifting his head, pinching a cigarette from his thin, chapped lips before throwing it into the doorway. His eyes were fixed on me. The cigarette hissed onto the broken drainpipe that leans precariously at the edge of our doorstep. Incandescent flecks of ash fizzed brightly into the chilly night air, orange and fleeting, their heat tamed by the cold.

And still he stared.

Then, hands in pockets, he came towards us. He walked straight towards *me*. My guts tightened and my heart battered against my chest. He got to within an inch of my face before eyeing me up and down, with an assurance that wrenched away any ounce of purpose I still possessed. And in my head I answered him.

Yes, this is all I am.

There was no reality, just a dreamy haze, an uncomfortable air, a sleepy violence, anxious and stirring. I'd never felt so unready for anything, yet so sure of something, in my life.

Then he hit me.

It was a thunderous head-butt that smacked into my face, full on the nose. He didn't even have the common decency to remove his fists from the warmth of his pockets. It was a muffled thud, to which I rocked back in my stance, jolting unsteadily. A narrow tweak of pain rushed through my body, flicking every nerve in its path before piercing the pit of my skull. It was a scything, splitting ache that tangled itself around my slippery hold on reality, teasing and tormenting my vision. I could sense a thin trickle of blood run into the corner of my mouth. I could taste blood. My nose was visibly throbbing, like a siren, an alarm. My face was puffing up, my eyes closing. I felt dizzy, uncertain, but no longer cold.

Then he spoke. I really didn't want him to talk to me. As it was he struck a vicious blow to my nose without me even so much as acknowledging him, let alone saying anything untoward or disagreeable. The fact he was talking to me probably meant he wanted me to talk back. Imagine the punishment dished out for upsetting him? What if I said the wrong thing or the right thing or didn't say enough or said too much or didn't say anything at all?

'It's rude to stare. Didn't your bitch of a mother ever tell you that, son?'

His face was so close I could feel every spoken word. I looked straight at him, not in any foolish attempt at bravado but because I didn't want another whack for not paying attention. This proved difficult however, due to the fact that my eyes were blurred with a heady mix of pain and water, and the conjoining of blood and mucus in my nose were adding to my general lack of composure. I had sobered from the alcohol but was now disoriented by shock and hurt.

I squeezed together every fragile strand of consciousness I still owned, and focused on his face. He was ghostly white, almost grey, his head made up of lumps and bumps, like a cobbled street. His features were worn and weathered, his shaven scalp marked and scarred like a shark. One of his eyes opened wider than the other and his teeth were small and misshapen, yellow and black, anything but pure white. Some of his teeth were broken or chipped and there was a glint of gold in amongst the foul grime of his mouth.

The stench of nicotine was sickly, his breath grisly and monstrous. As his lips parted, a foamy grub of spittle stretched between them, clinging like a bar on a prison window, made from his fetid saliva, barely protecting me from the gamy contents of his mouth. Through the long black look in his eye I could almost see his shrivelled soul. His air was that of a brutish animal. He leant into my left ear and began to growl. I could hear his breath, gruff and sinister. His whole demeanour was one of sheer inelegance and I felt sick, right through to my stomach. I was shaking. Uncontrollably. And the more I tried to stop, the more I twitched and pulsed.

As he spoke again, every chilling word rattled through me, his voice grating, like he was rubbing my nerve-endings on the jagged edge of a broken bottle.

'Now you kids better run along before I start handing out the real stuff. This ain't no pub brawl or schoolboy rumble in the playground. You've stumbled across some serious shit and you're stopping me do my job. No one stops me doing my job. If you try, I'll break you. So I suggest you piss off somewhere else before I really lose my rag. Say nothing, do nothing. Just fuck off. *Now.*'

It was a dark growl, hoarse and stiff, except the 'now' bit; that was bawled sharply, making me jump. I guess that was the idea, his thirst for control being unquenchable. Then he smiled, if you can call it a smile. It was as if he'd read the instructions on how to smile but was too stupid or nasty to understand them properly. I figured there wasn't much we could do for the girl from this position. There were six of them and three of us. We were normal, regular, daytime people. They weren't. It wasn't a case of a few meaty fellas who liked to bend back the old arm, who enjoyed a good set-to. These guys got paid for doing this, it was their job, you could just tell. The way they looked, the way they moved, the way they spoke; fear wasn't an option, compassion wasn't an option. And although hassling a defenceless woman is anything but proof of a man's physical strength, it was more than enough evidence that they were professional heavies, hired muscle, without a moral barometer between the lot of them. I didn't have to get head-butted to be convinced of this. Sharkhead did that anyway, for kicks, perk of the job. We were no physical threat to them, simply an uncalculated nuisance, like flies in need of swatting.

Still, despite stumbling across something sinister and complicated, we had been given the opportunity to get out without tasting any more violence. I, for one, intended to grab that opportunity with both hands. The way I saw it, we could run, find somewhere safe, phone the police and get home in one piece – no funny business, no death-wish-heroics, no broken kneecaps, no bother. The fact that neither Connor nor Donnie had jumped to my defence when Sharkhead butted me led me to assume that no conference was necessary. It would be a unanimous decision, in the bag, bought and paid for. Connor detests violence. Well, he detests *real*

33

violence. He's a gentle soul who only gets near a fight if it's on cable TV and he's paid for it, that or a gangster movie. He loves gangster movies. He's a big fan of screen violence but, like Donnie and I, has an issue with members of London's underground mafia carrying out all manner of bloody vengeance on our doorstep. I'm sure they'd both agree with me when I say that the ugly face of crime had no business sniffing around here. It was all far too close for comfort.

I only ever recall Connor getting properly riled once. He beat the shit out of this kid at school after he called his dad an Irish bastard, suggesting they, as a family, piss off back to Ireland with all the other spud pickers and terrorists. Connor was thirteen years old and new at school. And had just lost his dad to cancer.

Connor usually wins his battles with banter. But this particular kid, at this particular time and on this particular subject made something snap inside him. Connor battered the little bully to tears as the rest of the lunchtime crowd looked on in gleeful amazement. He was like an animal. And that is the only time I've seen Connor anything other than the placid pacifist that stood quivering beside me right then. And he wasn't about to try the same thing with these maniacs, Irish bastard or not.

As for Donnie, he can get quite feisty on the rugby field but, despite his ample frame, regards violence as no answer. This is in stark contrast to his father, Bob, who once swore by it as a tonic for most work-related problems. Suffice to say, there's a fair bit of skullduggery in the bloodline, but Donnie tends to baulk against it, choosing instead to do his own thing. Indeed, none of us are the type to sign up for street brawls with psychopaths. But then again, who the hell is? No one I've ever wanted as a friend anyway. Until then, that is.

So I assumed I could speak for the group as a whole when I decided to grasp the opportunity to walk when it was offered. Just being *able* to walk was a blessing right now. So I nodded, trying to portray an even greater amount of fear than I actually felt. Which wasn't easy. But I suspected he was the kind of guy who gets off on stuff like that, scaring people, hitting people, that sort of thing. Because my face was so numb with pain and with cold, I was concerned that, when I did eventually muster enough energy and courage to speak, I may end up spraying blood and gunk all over the face and clothes of a man who had just head-butted me for standing outside my own front door. If the punishment fits the crime then soiling his leather trench coat could eventuate in me donning concrete boots and doing the old midnight swim at the bottom of the Thames, along with the floating toiletries and discarded supermarket trolleys. So I went for damage limitation. I mumbled. And as I mumbled I kept my head down. With chin glued tight to chest, I slowly uttered what was fast becoming the most awkward sentence of my life.

'We're going, *we're going.* '

I repeated myself, in case he didn't hear me the first time, and I held my hands up too, just to compound my show of surrender. The second *'we're going'* was a bit more squeaky and exasperated than the first. I felt it important to come across as weak and cowardly as possible. This wasn't too difficult; deep down I felt very weak and extremely cowardly and, at that moment, it was infinitely preferable to feeling more pain.

I started to walk - well, not walk exactly - more shuffle. I started to shuffle towards the pavement. I sneaked a quick glance over my left shoulder to make sure the other two were aware of my movement ... and yes, they were. They were shuffling too. We were getting out of this with one minor injury and should be able to save the girl in the process. Whatever they were going to do, they couldn't do it here and they couldn't do it now.

On my way past I caught a glimpse of one of the other men. He had long curly hair, dragged back into a ponytail. A few rogue strands were left swinging about in a bitter wind that, every so often, built up into a frenzy, swirling around the doorway, spewing all manner of debris around him, causing him to flinch and cover his face with the arm that wasn't attached to the girl. Two of the other men kept looking around, constantly scouring, never at us, always around and around, scanning and peering into the black and blue of night. Another was lighting up, his face obscured by a wave of chilled breath and cigarette smoke, swirling angrily, following him as he moved towards the next man. He was big, even in this company, and hovered over us like a shadow, still as night, except for the eyes. As we moved so did his glare, like a couple of heat-seeking missiles.

The place was dead. This whole situation was unfortunate in so many ways, but especially because no one was likely to see us. This was *our* doorway, leading up to *our* flat, the only other person that may use this doorway would be a burglar, and we had quite enough trouble without bumping into another miscreant. So unless you lived here, you wouldn't venture this far from the road. If they wanted somewhere dead quiet, they'd found it.

On we went, crunching awkwardly over the gravel pathway, tiny stones gripping our footing, everything unsteady, uneasy. Then onto the fissured pavement where fine cracks splintered the concrete, catching dirt, cigarette butts and all the grime from the street.

We moved towards the safety of the road.

And still he glared.

We were out.

We were on the road.

First me, then Connor, then . . . Donnie turned round. Not only did he turn round, he said something. Then they darted for us, pouncing like alley cats, from window ledge to dustbin, like it was the most natural thing in the world, their eyes glinting, savage and untamed. They hooked and scratched and smartly overwhelmed our feeble efforts to escape their white-knuckle clutches. We were grabbed, gripped and dragged. Dragged back to where we'd just been, to the place where no one else goes. It was so quick we hardly had time to even think about running. One by one we were shoved down onto the gravel path and pulled towards the doorway. The loose shingle scraped on my back, lacerating against cold raw skin. My head bounced off the pavement catching the bridge of my battered and inflamed nose. My guts twisted and my mouth filled with all manner of debris. Connor and Donnie were reduced to a blurry black shadow, swirling alongside me. My senses were jammed. Winter's blustery clasp was grappling a very slender hold on reality.

We were bundled down the alley at the side of our doorway and then along towards the garages.

Then we stopped.

Then they said they'd kill us.

Then they started to kill Connor.

And there wasn't a single thing we could do about it.

6
Sunday: 00:21 am

'**H**ow about letting the girl go now, guys? Not exactly a fair fight is it?'

That's what Donnie said. I'll never forget it. At the time I didn't know what he'd said. I just knew he'd said something and I knew it meant we should run. The moment I knew his exact words was when they were repeated to me by Sharkhead, whilst being held so tightly round the throat I wondered where my next breath was coming from. And he said them with such a heavy, sardonic tone that I began to fear for our lives.

That head-butt was inflicted despite the lack of anything that could be deemed provocative. Suddenly Donnie had not only turned around and said something; he'd questioned their judgment, undermining a sense of authority that was obviously important to them. The outlook was gloomy to say the least. I couldn't believe it. Chivalry might be dead but I sure as hell didn't want to die trying to revive it. We were no use to this girl now. We were just male versions of her.

Sharkhead turned his attention to Donnie. He spoke with a mixture of disbelief, annoyance and plain old viciousness.

'Seeing as you care so much for this bitch, I'll gladly show you what we were going do to her before you stuck your fucking noses in. And I'll show you by doing the exact same fucking thing to one of your mates. Because if you gave a shit about them, you'd have pissed off and kept your fucking mouth shut. You're the big man, eh? We'll see about that. We'll see how big you feel after you've watched your pal get beaten to death in front of your own fucking eyes. And then, when you've seen that, we'll do the same to you.'

As he spoke his eyes flickered, reflecting the dull orange glow of a distant street lamp, a light that was too weak and too far away to be of any use to us now. All it did was add the colour of fire to his glare.

It was the look of someone on the verge of violence.

And that was it.

No more talking.

They say actions speak louder than words, what followed was the personification of that saying. If you've ever been held down by a couple of men twice your size whilst they force you to witness one of your best mates get the living hell beaten out of him, then you'll know that particular image is unforgettable. You'll be aware of how physically ill it makes you feel; how your stomach grips; how the tears roll from your eyes; how the anger rolls and coils inside you and how that overriding feeling of helplessness builds with every sickening blow. The hatred was boiling inside me but it had no release; so it just turned and sank, deeper inside.

That's why those sick bastards did it that way. It would have been logical to start with Donnie; after all it was him who had shouted back at them. But they play these games for a living. They wanted to throw a few warped lessons in for good measure. By starting with the most innocent, the one with the slightest build and the most fear in his eyes, they were inflicting all sorts of pain in one go. And they were enjoying it too; you could see it in their eyes.

If it were happening on one of Connor's gangster movies then we'd be admiring both their cruelness and their coolness. But it wasn't. This was real. It was horrible, devastating and grossly unfair, but it was still real. Connor was being punched and kicked by men who didn't care that they'd never met him before or that he hadn't done anything wrong or that he was one of the nicest, funniest, most tender people they'd ever come across. And they didn't give a damn that he was, after all these years, still coming to terms with the death of his father. His hero. He was being punched and kicked by men who did so with cigarettes still in their mouths. They loved it, every nauseating second. And all I could do was watch, helpless, frustrated, out of control.

I had to do something.

The more I struggled, the tighter the grip, like handcuffs. It could only have been thirty seconds but they laid so many blows into Connor I thought he was going to die. I searched deep for ideas but was empty. Held in a suffocating headlock, I looked over to Donnie and saw that he too was being held in a headlock, being forced to watch. But he didn't appear to be struggling. Instead he just sat on his knees and stared at the tragedy unfolding in front of him. He was taking his punishment because it was all he could do.

My eyes were momentarily diverted by a distant set of car headlamps. A weak, watery spray of off-white light shone through one of the overgrown hedges that loosely line our gravel driveway. I could see the night's soft drizzle illuminate as the vehicle brushed past the foliage that stood between safety and us. I could also see potential, hope even. So I decided to shout. It wasn't much of a plan but it was all I could think of given the circumstances. I wasn't even sure if I was physically capable of shouting. Such was the bizarre and nightmarish feel to all of this, I half-expected to try and shout, only to find I had lost my voice, like in the scary dream of a child.

My plan would either speed up the intensity of violence or introduce a little confusion. I figured it was worth the risk. So I bellowed out, as loud as humanly possible. I shouted the one word that might prevent them from killing my friend, the one thing that may induce a state of mild concern or, better still, slight panic. I took a deep breath, gathered all the exasperation and aggression that had seized my every muscle and I cried out, *'POLICE!'*

And it worked.

They didn't exactly panic but the combination of the car headlights and the possibility of the police proved distraction enough. They stopped and looked at each other, then scattered their gaze all around, swinging like prison spotlights. I waited for the grip around my neck to loosen slightly and when it did I jumped. I elbowed the man holding me in the head. He cupped his face and yelped. I started shouting and ran towards Connor. There was definitely a state of chaos building, just enough to allow Donnie to struggle free too.

And when he did, he went mad, diving headfirst on the pony-tailed man who, just seconds earlier, had been relentlessly booting Connor's static heap in the guts.

Donnie completely pummelled him, landing blow after blow to his head, a quite devastating attack. One of the others tried to grab hold of him but he just brushed him off, clouting him round the jaw with a huge right fist. Donnie used every inch of himself in exacting some painful justice. It came straight from the family photo album, blind, intrinsic, lethal. The vital difference: he wasn't enjoying it.

As for me, I kicked one in the groin and jumped on another. I think I may even have bitten someone. But Donnie was chief. He was enraged, empowered by a hatred that had simmered and bubbled but was now boiling over. He'd found energy and strength where guilt and pain had accrued, paralysing him. He'd been forced to watch the beating of his friend like it was some sick personal concert, for his benefit. Now the floor was his. And he was putting on quite a show.

These strangers had dragged us into their world and we weren't going down without a fight. I was determined to do something, to make my mark – a bloodied lip, a scar, ripped shirt, dented pride, wounded ego, anything that could somehow re-address the balance and make up for what they'd done to Connor. But there was no way we could match them. There was no way we could win. And, judging by the state of Connor, there was no way we could even come close. But we were hoping the distraction itself might prove enough. It was our only hope, and Connor's only hope. We were praying the commotion would save our friend, and if that meant Donnie cracking a few skulls, then so much the better. But they quickly overpowered us. At least the girl got away. In all the panic she ran screaming, petrified and grateful for a chance to flee what was fast becoming a crazed battleground. Her instinct was good; she saw a hole in the night and scrambled through it.

The atmosphere had altered. They were back in control but their prisoner had gone. And with her had gone their reason for being here. As a result, they couldn't react to our plucky rebellion in the way they would have liked. In other words they would have to let us off the hook. We simply weren't worth it. The commotion had inevitably taken its toll and the street was starting to react to the strange goings-on. The comfortable silence that normally shrouds our road after midnight had been pierced. Curtains began to twitch, windows started to light up and the faraway cry of dissenting neighbours punctuated the night sky.

There was a brief scuffle but nothing like the savage treatment Connor had received. We were picked up, pushed about a bit, then thrown to the ground. It was all they had time for. It was time for this mob to ship out. The likes of us were never worth a flirtation with the authorities and as quickly as they had appeared, they were gone, scurrying away, like sewer rats dispersing into the black of night. There was a distant screech of tyres and then silence. We picked up Connor's ravaged frame and took him down to the roadside. I scrambled around for my mobile and prayed it was still working. It was. Connor's had shattered in his pocket, such was the severity of his beating. I called for an ambulance. Donnie tried to talk to Connor, his voice quivering with fear. But there was no reaction. The only movement coming from Connor was that steady flow of blood.

Faced with that gutter I sat down beside Connor's lifeless body. I placed my hand on his back and pleaded with God to keep my friend alive.

7
Sunday morning, 8:17 am

'**I** thought I could reason with them, you know. It just didn't seem right leaving that girl on the brink of getting her head smashed in. Or even worse.'

Donnie was parking the car in the hospital car park. He'd managed to get a spot right outside the main entrance and normally he'd be boring me about how good it was. I don't think he even noticed how good the parking spot was. He was far too preoccupied.

I'd called the hospital from the car and we were both relieved to hear that Connor, though battered and bruised, was awake and relatively comfortable. When we'd left him in the early hours he was barely able to talk. The nurse said we could see him for a short while despite the time. Which was big of her. She also informed me that he was a very lucky young man. I didn't quite know how to take this comment but decided to let it slide. It annoyed me because from where I was sitting Connor had been pretty *un*lucky. The nurse had obviously assumed he'd been involved in some mindless drunken scuffle over a spilt pint or a wandering elbow or an unsubtle gawk at someone else's girlfriend. I couldn't be bothered to explain that her

46

condescending manner, blatant lack of professionalism and inaccurate summation were both inappropriate and very irritating. I guess she'd spent too many Saturday night shifts patching up incoherent males amongst a haze of stale booze. I was just glad that Connor was okay, that he was alive.

Meanwhile Donnie was being eaten alive by a crescendo of guilt and fear. The nearer we got to the hospital entrance the more he fumbled, fidgeted and stuttered, a crumbling shadow of his proper self. For anyone to be scared of Connor was laughable, but for Donnie it was unthinkable. I just wanted everything to be like it was. However much I tried to assure Donnie that it would all be okay, I couldn't help thinking that he *had* messed up a bit, that he had, in a way, let Connor down, and subsequently played a major role in tossing all our lives around. Reason with them? One of them had just head-butted me. How do you reason with that? Something had possessed him to struggle for fair-mindedness, to shun the brutality that stirred around him, to find compassion where there clearly was none. Maybe he was recoiling from his father's past. Who knows? All I knew was that last night wasn't the forum for that. But again I didn't argue; he was suffering enough. I just hoped Connor was in a forgiving mood.

The automatic doors swished open and that clinical waft ghosted towards us.

'Shit,' Donnie said, stopping in his tracks.

His panicking was now infuriating me.

'We haven't brought anything, Sam. What kind of people visit their sick friend in hospital without so much as a bag of grapes?'

What kind of person gets his friend beaten up because he couldn't keep his stupid mouth shut? It's going to take more than a few nice treats to get out of this one.

'Good point Donnie; a few nice treats should do the trick.'

'Do you reckon he'd appreciate a porno mag?'

'Do they sell them in hospitals?'

'Dunno. It's not like it's a church.'

'But what if he can't, you know, take full advantage of it. Pretty frustrating gift if he's not able to, you know; can you imagine?'

The thought that simultaneously entered our heads was enough to send the walls of apprehension and pointless blame crashing down. The vision of Connor being too bound up to pleasure himself despite the arrival of a pile of skin mags sent us both into hysterics – not a great look considering we were in a hospital foyer, surrounded by wheelchairs and worried relatives. But, for that moment, we didn't care. And I think that that brief conversation compounded how strongly we felt for the person we were about to see. Donnie spent a small fortune in the shop, mostly on crap, what with it being Sunday and all. Then we boarded the lift before walking slowly through a couple of glossy, cold corridors until we reached Connor's ward.

And there he was.

In the very corner, all stitched-up, taped and bandaged, was our Connor. We moved towards him before stopping suddenly. He wasn't alone. There were three people with him, two men and a woman. And he was sitting up, talking to them. Neither of us had any idea who they were nor what they were doing here. Call it paranoia, over-protection or a natural consequence of last night, but I didn't like it. After being bitten once I was now feeling incredibly shy. Furthermore the two men hovering over Connor were as equally tough looking as those from last night. They weren't the same people but were just as menacing. I was caught between darting to my friend's side and legging it in the opposite direction. So I stopped, gathered myself, then skulked back round the corner.

'Who the hell are they?' Donnie whispered.

He was standing in front of me, holding my arm, as if trying to take some belated sense of control.

'How the hell should I know?' I snapped.

'Well, they're not the blokes from last night.'

'Police?'

'Nah, too dodgy-looking.'

'What about the girl?'

'Yeah, she's … well, tasty.'

'No, who is she?'

'Oh. Dunno.'

'He's clocked us.'

'Shit!'

'Let's go. Oh, and Donnie?'

'What?'

'Don't say anything stupid. I know you feel bad about everything but try and avoid the old foot-in-gob thing you do sometimes when you're nervous.'

'Okay, okay. I'll be fine.'

'Right.'

'Jesus Christ, Connor, look at the state of your bloody face.'

I felt confused and unsettled. Connor's face *was* a mess, all puffed-up and bruised. He had a stitched-up gash over his left eye and the other was purple and swollen. There were several bandages stretched tightly round his waist and numerous scratches over his face and upper body. But he was sat up and he was talking, which spelt progress of sorts.

He looked up and smiled, typically upbeat, making us feel even worse.

'Cheer up, fellas. I wasn't that good looking in the first place. Besides, I should be due a few sympathy shags now, what do you reckon?'

'Not quite yet, pal,' said one of the scary bedside strangers.

He was shortish, heavily built, all pecs and shoulders and no real neck to speak of. And he had one of those permanent frowns that add a menacing edge to the most benign of comments. His droll quip led the other one - taller, more sinewy - to release a deep growl of acknowledgement that I'm sure was an authentic laugh in a previous life. The way Connor reacted you'd think he'd just won a comedian of the decade award. He damn near split his stitches.

I smiled and made a point of averting my curious glare away from them. Despite being desperate to find out who they were, I had, very recently, learnt that there were some eye-lines that weren't worth catching. One of them moved towards us. It was the girl. I couldn't help but return her gaze. She seemed familiar. And then it came to me. It was her. It was the girl from last night, minus the hand around her throat. She smiled fleetingly, embarrassed almost.

Then Connor introduced her: 'Guys, I'd like you to meet Tony and Mick Taylor, and their sister, Jodie. You've sort of met Jodie before. This is Sam and Donnie; the other two.'

'Nice to meet you, again,' I said to Jodie, keen to sound neither overly familiar nor annoyingly aloof, but somewhere in between the two. And as I said it I wondered what it would take to tip these guys over the verge. I wondered what they deemed worthy of a judicious gesture of violence. However, nothing untoward happened so I leant over and shook her hand.

'You, too,' she replied. 'Listen, I just wanted to say thanks and, you know, sorry. I can't believe what went on last night. I'm sorry you lot got dragged into it. But I'm also very grateful. It's so unfair on poor Connor but I'm glad you were around. God knows what would have happened if … well, anyway. You were all very brave. Thank you.'

'That goes for us, too, fellas.'

This was Tony, the short, stocky one with the square jaw and the gloomy voice, a voice echoing the terror of last night.

'You saved our kid sister and for that we're very grateful. You don't need to know the ins and outs of it all. It's safer for you that way. Besides, it's all a bit complicated. Those men will pay; you can rest assured of that. We know who they are. They've gone too far this time. You done us a good turn and we owe you, we owe you big time. If there's anything we can do in return, you name it.'

I listened and nodded, but couldn't help thinking that the best thing he could do for us right now was to leave us in peace. Whatever world we'd stumbled into yesterday I didn't want to re-visit it today. The more I looked the more I realised there was no difference between these two and the six from last night: same world, same violence, same fear. I didn't want to be tangled up in it, suffocated by his gratitude. Rest assured? Yeah right. I wanted to stand there and tell this bloke to shove his thanks. I wanted to let him know that I wasn't the least bit interested in what last night was about; that I was sure it was seedy, desperate and utterly barbaric.

But I didn't.

I didn't tell him because I was sick of upsetting people who got upset so easily, of pushing people who lived on the edge, people who walked a tightrope between anger and violence. I didn't want to be the one to unhinge him. Besides, he was thanking me, he owed me, and he was probably being as civil and gracious as he had ever been to a complete stranger in his life. Yet I was still scared of him. I wasn't impressed or flattered, just plain old scared. And I was adamant that I never wanted to call in that favour, that I never wanted to see them again as long as I lived.

However, I was glad we'd been able to help the girl, Jodie. She seemed, on first impression, as stuck as we were. I felt a little sorry for her. Not as sorry as I did for Connor, but sorry nevertheless. I pitied her situation. She seemed ill at ease, appearing to rebel against her brothers' talk of fights, foes and revenge. She may well have been dragged reluctantly into all of this, like us. But it would be hard for her to escape. Not only could she not choose her family, but her enemies had been chosen for her too.

Tony and Mick Taylor shook our hands. They were taut, tense handshakes. Unlike their sister they did not apologise directly, nor were they the least bit shocked by the state of Connor. This was the nature of their business; they weren't going to start apologising for that. Besides, they were far too busy plotting a revenge attack, one that involved more blood and more pain no doubt. I guess that's how they determine relative success in their business; the ones who relinquish the least amount of blood are the winners.

They lifted the collars of their jackets, patted Connor on the shoulder, nodded sternly and walked away in search of bloody vengeance. Out of our faces and out of our world. For good? Judging by Connor's positive reaction to them, I couldn't help thinking we'd be seeing their sort again.

8
Sunday: 8:46 am

As the Taylors departed, so the anxiety slid away. Donnie sat on the chair by Connor's side and I perched myself on the edge of the bed. Finally it was just the three of us again.

Me: 'So, what's the damage?'

Connor: 'A load of bruising and a battered ego.'

Me: 'That all? Hardly any point coming then!'

Connor: 'Could have been a lot worse. It'll be a while before I'm busting some serious moves on the dance floor but it feels good to be alive. Besides, few days off work, afternoon kips, I'm sure there's a silver-lining there somewhere.'

Me: 'But what are your actual injuries?'

Connor: 'I lost a fair bit of blood, bit of concussion, cracked a couple of ribs; it was this cut above my eye that was bleeding the worst apparently. There's a fair few stitches in it, but I'll be okay. I've got a thick head, me.'

Me: 'Scary stuff though, Con. You had us worried there for a while.'

Connor: 'I was giving them a few free shots. Like Rocky used to. I was just about to start fighting back

54

when I got hit with a lucky left hook. Still, they'll keep. So, come on Don, let's have it.'

Donnie: 'Right. Sure. Look, Con, I'm really, really sorry, mate. I don't know what came over me, I *really* ...

Connor: 'Not an apology, you silly prick. The bag. Hand over the goods. I presume that's for me and I also presume it's jam-packed full of treats, so let's have it.'

Donnie: 'Right, sure, no worries, Con. But about last night ... '

Connor: 'So what have we here? Plenty of crisps - excellent - fizzy drinks, chocolate, kids' sweets, Sunday papers - nice one. It's all there. Good effort, boys. You've excelled yourselves. I take it they don't sell porn down there then?'

Donnie: 'Seriously Con, I'm so sorry about everything ... '

Connor: 'Forget it, Donnie. It's okay. If this is what it takes to save the girl then, hey, who am I to argue? Shit happens. I'm stiil here, so let's leave it. You're starting to embarrass yourself now. It's not a good look.'

Me: 'So how are you really feeling?'

Connor: 'Very sore. A bit weird really, you know.'

Me: 'That's understandable.'

Connor: 'It's strange though, those guys coming to see me. Quite a thrill, really, in a funny sort of way.'

Donnie: 'What do you mean?'

Connor: 'Don't tell me you don't know who those blokes are?'

Me: 'Haven't got a clue, mate.'

Connor: 'You're jesting with me, right? You're having a laugh. They're the fucking *Taylors*.'

Me: 'Yeah, well, I sort of gathered that by the fact you introduced them as Tony and Mick *Taylor*.'

Connor: 'For God's sake, boys. I think there's a couple of villages missing their idiots right about now.'

Donnie: 'Are they famous or something?'

Connor: 'Don't you read the papers? They're only *the* Taylor brothers.'

Me: 'We're going round in circles a bit here, Con. Concussion is a terrible thing, I know, but could you please tell us who the bloody Taylors are?'

Connor: 'Yes, they're famous. Or should I say infamous.'

Me: 'Are they gangsters or something?'

Connor: 'Shit yeah. Cool huh?'

Me: 'No.'

Donnie: 'Well, maybe a little.'

Me: 'Please don't go there, Don. Look at the state of him; there's absolutely nothing cool about this.'

Connor: 'Calm down Grandad.'

Me: 'Alright, alright. So who are they?'

Connor: 'They're mad bastards, mate; well-hard geezers, into all sorts of shit: drugs, nightclubs, strip joints, protection rackets, loads of dodgy dealings. They've been on the news and stuff. There was a big furore a while back when one of them was put on the board of a football club.'

Donnie: 'Actually, that does ring a bell. That was the elder brother, wasn't it?'

Connor: 'Yeah, Danny Taylor. He's not into the heavy stuff anymore; retired from the gangster business a while back. He's old school. You know, just did proper crimes, heists, raids, post office jobs, sawn-off shotguns, that sort of thing.'

Me: 'Very admirable, I'm sure. So who were the other guys last night?'

Connor: 'They're the O'Donnell's, another dodgy family business, with designs on the Taylor's patch over this side of the city. The feud goes way back. They hate each other. We obviously interrupted something. I don't know much more, they were a bit coy about the finer details, not the sort of dudes you can coax information out of, unless you want your drum torched.'

Me: 'Trust us to bump into the bloody Goodfellas.'

Connor: 'I know. Very exciting.'

Me: 'Not really. These blokes sound like full-on mental cases. You haven't told them anything about yourself have you?'

Connor: 'Of course not. It is a *bit* impressive, though. I mean, the book I'm reading at the moment actually mentions these blokes in it. They're well known players from way back, proper London mafia faces, proper fucking gangsters. And they were thanking *me*.'

Me: 'Yeah, well, you could have died last night. This is all miles away from the movies and the books and all the glamour stuff, Con.'

Connor: 'Settle down.'

Me: 'Besides, what were they doing over here? I thought those guys got nosebleeds if they stray too far out the East End.'

Connor: 'From what I could gather, Jodie, the sister, lives over this way. She isn't part of the business. I guess she's an easy target. Not bad looking though?'

Donnie: 'Very acceptable. I was seriously contemplating grabbing her number; glad I didn't now.'

Me: 'You'd be mad to even look at a girl like that. Her brothers would spoon your eyes out. Not that you're interested in other girls anymore, Don.'

Donnie: 'Piss off.'

Me: 'I guess that explains why there were so many of them last night.'

Connor: 'Yeah. Talk about overkill, six blokes against one girl. I think the O'Donnells were making a statement. Well, they were until we showed up. The Taylor boys aren't too happy about last night, you can tell. Someone's going to pay, big time.'

Me: 'Who cares, as long as we don't have to get involved.'

Connor: 'By the state of your hands, Don, you got a little involved yourself.'

Donnie: 'Too little, too late, I'm afraid, Con.'

Connor: 'Well, I appreciate the effort. Went a bit Travis Bickle did we, or was it more of a Pesci / DeNiro effort? Chip off the old block, eh?'

Donnie: 'No, not at all, that's not really my style, mate, you know that. Have the police been to see you yet?'

Connor: 'The nurse said they were sniffing about last night but I was in no fit state to talk. I expect they'll come back today.'

Me: 'Make sure you tell them everything.'

Connor: 'I'm no grass. You've gotta keep shtum in this game. Otherwise you end up getting knee-capped.'

Me: 'This doesn't make you a gangster, Con. Just an unlucky bastard.'

Connor: 'I know.'

Me: 'Good.'

Donnie: 'You look knackered, mate.'

Connor: 'I feel a bit dodgy, actually. Think the painkillers are wearing off.'

Donnie: 'Do you want me to fetch a nurse?'

Connor: 'Yeah, cheers.'

Donnie: 'We'll leave you to get some sleep.'

Connor: 'Listen guys. Thanks for coming. And thanks for the goodies. They reckon I'll be in for a few days so could you call work for me?

Donnie: 'No worries. How *will* Kathy manage without you?'

Connor: *'Piss off!'*

Donnie: 'Hey, Con. Thanks for not throwing the big guilt trip on me. I appreciate it.'

Connor: 'Mate, you always put chicks first, we're used to it.'

Donnie: 'Steady.'

Connor: 'Don't worry. At least I met the Taylors.'

Me: 'I'm not sure that's such a good thing.'

Donnie: 'How did they know you were here anyway?'

Connor: 'Doesn't take a genius to work out where I was going. It was a toss up between here and the morgue by the sound of it. Shit, Sam, I almost forgot. You'll never guess who I saw earlier.'

Me: 'Al Capone?'

Connor: 'Funny man.'

Me: 'Who then?'

Connor: 'Someone you used to get on *very* well with. Back at school.'

Me: 'Tell me.'

Connor: 'There's no need to, she's standing right behind you.'

It was Abby.

It was Abby North, my first proper girlfriend, from school, from way back.

'Hi Sam.'

'Abby, what are you doing here?'

'I'm a nurse.'

'Right. Of course, hospitals and all that.'

'Nose looks sore.'

'Yeah, big night out.'

'Apart from that though, you still look pretty good.'

'*Do I?* I mean, do I? Thanks, cheers. So do you. Nice outfit.'

'I'm a nurse, Sam, not a stripper.'

'I know, I know.'

'Fancy a coffee, I've just finished night shift?'

'Coffee sounds good.'

'It's good to see you, Sam.'

'Thanks. You too, Abby.'

And with that, she leant over and hugged me. It was a slightly awkward embrace, twitchy, robotic, standoffish, but friendly enough and not altogether inappropriate. I hadn't seen Abby North since our last summer at school, over seven years ago. I'd gone off to uni, she'd gone off to nursing college, and that was it, except for the first weekend after uni started. I went back, she went back, eventually we weaned ourselves off each other, wove ourselves a new life. It never really ended, just faded, like a hickie.

I introduced her to Donnie and, based on personality and track record, half-expected them to start bonking on the admin desk at the front of Connor's ward. But it seemed Abby was more interested in me than my Australian friend, which, including Nicole, made a grand total of two. Once she'd realised he'd lived here

60

for the past four and a half years and therefore couldn't tell her what was happening in *Home and Away*, she focused on me, and in particular, my nose. She said it looked broken but, beyond painkillers and work avoidance, there was little I could do as far as treatment goes.

She looked well, a tad larger in the breast and hip department than I remembered, although that may have been the outfit. Her hair, like so many others these days, had been lightened from mouse brown to somewhere near blonde. She was still pretty, still funny and we spent the next twenty minutes re-acquainting over a pot of English Breakfast, picking up on the past.

It was all very agreeable. Her wit was as sharp and risqué as ever, and I hoped it wouldn't be another seven years between meetings. She'd helped me forget, for a moment at least, the events of the recent past, allowing me instead to stretch back time, de-magnify the present. And it led me to wondering. The sense of romance had long since petered out, those feelings trapped in the class of '92 photo that lines a box in my mum's attic, forever eclipsed by the years with Nicole. But I felt sure I could benefit from having a proper female friend. I'd not really had one of those since school. They'd always been girlfriends of friends or work colleagues, reliant on the whims of others and the weave of fate, with no glue or history to speak of. So as she left for her post-shift sleep, I made a mental list of the benefits of inter-gender friendship: there was the free insider trading, the smug sense of maturity, the cheaper rounds and, most exciting of all, the advice on how to win back my ex-girlfriend.

As a direct result of this breakthrough, I sensed a slight upturn in my mood. Connor had looked dreadful, but still better than the broken wreck of a man that lay strewn on the pavement at midnight. Donnie also appeared brighter, safe in the knowledge that Connor had no interest in apportioning blame. But again he neglected to mention the stellar parking spot.

Things weren't quite back to normal.

And I sensed it would be a while before they were.

9
Sunday: 10:07 am

Question: What do you the day after a night like that?
Answer: Retail therapy.

There's no point working all week if you can't enjoy the fruits of your labour come the weekend. I fancied a spot of self-pampering and hoped it would be the catalyst to further re-ignite my enthusiasm for life, inject a bit of zest into what was still a fairly weak and powdery spirit.

Sunday has always been a day for unwinding and strolling but recently has also become the official day for perusing and purchasing. The Bible Bashers are urinating against the wind if they think they can keep Sunday to themselves. They put up a decent fight for two thousand years but in the end crumbled under the heavy weight of commercialism. We've now divvied up the day of rest between the pious and the purchasers; Sunday morning for bells and singing and Sunday afternoon for pubs and shopping; a fair compromise in anyone's language.

Connor and I have lived in West London since the start of uni, where I met Donnie and introduced them to each other. Before this we lived in a trifling village on the outskirts of London, in the middle of nowhere. Forced to get the bus to school every morning, we ached for the day we could actually walk to decent shops. We were driven by the fear of being isolated in the cultural wilderness, a place so sleepy it was impossible to find a pulse, less likely a heart. Hamesly-on-Thames. It was a village that, despite lying within spitting distance of the capital, held a blind refusal to acknowledge the positive aspects of London, spurning it with the kind of haughtiness that left us itching for the lights. They didn't like the way the city kept creeping towards them, like a nagging truth, a storm cloud ready to unload all the scum of the city onto their pompous little hedgerows, in front of their prying little eyes.

The irony being that when I was growing up just about every bloke in our village worked in London. Every weekday morning this army of little suits would exchange a cold kiss on the doormat before marching down to the train station like so many ants. They'd cram onto the London platform, avoiding eye contact, avoiding conversation and avoiding the drips of water that fell indiscriminately from the hanging baskets that dangled precariously in a brazen attempt to raise the profile of their station above those in town.

The coffee morning housewives would bemoan the fact they couldn't go to the opera these days without having to traipse around homeless kids. But the snobbery was worse, more pertinent, for my brother, Max, being gay and all. He and I were never that close as kids. It wasn't until we were adults that we started to forge a bit of brotherly love. It wasn't until then I realised he wasn't just the surly, aggressive older sibling I'd learnt to avoid, but, instead, a mixed-up adolescent living in a place where he didn't fit. The place suffocated him. Luckily I had Connor. Max had no one. Who could he turn to: his hoodlum mates, his depressed, pill-popping mother, his irksome little brother or a juvenile father who still thought your average poofter carried a handbag and said, 'ooh ducky'? That village was hardly a sanctuary for homosexual teenagers. The gay rights people tend to march around places like that. Max was into heavy metal. He liked the deafening noise and the negativity. He'd claim to spend his weekends in the city, fighting skinheads and watching rock bands. He didn't. He spent them down the park frightening kids and sniffing glue.

There were lots of secrets and lies in our village. Every so often a new scandal would rear up, tales of dirty tricks and business trips, lipstick on collars and guilt on consciences. The characters were always new but the narrative remained pretty constant. Then one day it was our turn.

I fled that village, the memories and the people, at the earliest opportunity, dashing off to uni with Connor. We met Donnie and, of course, I fell in love with Nicole. We travelled halfway round the world together, without a care, until the ghost of my family's past caught up with me, enjoyed a dubious fling with fate and left me where I am today, hanging on. Still I wanted them in my life. Both of them, my girlfriend and my father.

We had this huge row, Dad and I, about six months ago, when we first got back from Australia. It was a tough time; Nicole and I had begun our downward spiral when suddenly he fronts up with all this attitude and news. All the bad memories barged their way to the front of my head. I said some horrendous things and, at the time, think I meant them. I told him how his poor example had led me to react badly to the pregnancy; how he'd made me insecure, permanently fearful of responsibility, how he had a lot to answer for; what with the Peter Pan complex and the jumbo-sized ego, a crap male role model. I guess I was taking stuff out on him; it didn't make me feel any better, because, on the whole, it wasn't really true.

We used to be best friends. We were getting on okay too, until that blow out. I thought I'd feel better for it but in the end I didn't. I think it had been in my system for too long, warped with time, out of shape, gone stale. I felt bad about the whole thing but there was no way I was going to apologise. He never did. And, in fairness to me, his timing wasn't great. It was embarrassing, tactless and unnecessary. But then again, so was my reaction. I ruined his moment. The way I saw it, he'd ruined my life. Obviously that wasn't the case and I knew it even then. I just couldn't seem to help myself. When Nicole unravelled my past she did so with due care and attention. I saw the light and felt a warm glow, freeing my aching bones. I was happy again. But my happiness was reliant on there being two of us. Without the main ingredient it was a dish served cold and I'd been feeling the chill of loneliness ever since. Suddenly the highlight of my week was shopping for clothes and CDs on a wet Sunday at the end of winter.

Donnie didn't fancy being on his own so agreed to be dragged around the shops with me. Like all good toddlers in his position he promised not to moan as long as we got some nice food at the end of it. The plan was to shop a while before indulging in a late lunch in a

66

country pub somewhere. I liked the idea of poring over my purchases with a pint of lager and the promise of roast beef and Yorkshire pudding. Donnie agreed. We were hoping that that time-honoured combo of fresh air and a full belly would ease our mutual agitation.

My nose was proving an issue, both hampering my search for sartorial satisfaction and proving a constant reminder of the night before. Still, compared to Connor I was lucky. Donnie thought he sounded like he'd taken it all quite well. Personally, I thought he'd taken it all a bit *too* well. I was more worried about Connor's emotional scars than the physical ones. But I didn't tell Donnie this. I kept it to myself in the hope that I was wrong and he was right.

I wanted to get Connor a present, something to cheer him up. Many years ago I appointed myself his personal fashion guru. It's not an easy role. I always end up bartering with him because the difference between what he wants to spend and what passes for acceptable merchandise is often irredeemable. I ended up buying him a new shirt and a couple of T-shirts for myself, in the faint hope I'd be feeling warm again soon. The therapy was working but I needed something else, so, on Donnie's advice, set off towards one of the big department stores in search of something special.

And I got it.

So far it had been a fairly weird weekend, but it was about to enter the realms of the truly bizarre. A couple of hours after bumping into an old girlfriend on a hospital ward I heard the unmistakable voice of my ex-girlfriend, Nicole.

And, furthermore, I wasn't wearing any trousers.

10
Sunday, 1:02pm

I met Donnie in the second week of university. Like toddlers in a sandpit, we were instant friends, the same, simple agenda running between us, namely to meet as many drunk female students as possible.

And it was through Donnie I met Nicole, on a Tuesday night, which now, as a proper person, wouldn't strike me as more than a two pinter, but when you're at college, the social emphasis is on the middle of the week. And it was all happening in the Student Union that evening.

Connor, as was becoming commonplace, was sat in the corner of the room surrounded by a ring of acquiescent nerdy film buffs from his course. Donnie and I were at the bar, feeling generally superior, drenched in labels, financed by student loans. Rightly or wrongly, we felt a cut above the mishmash of badly dressed northerners and sheltered bumpkins who made up the majority of clientele in what was essentially a monumental dive. However, our fondness for the place soon grew, sparked initially by the quality of bar staff.

Donnie introduced me to the girl working behind the bar. He'd met her the weekend before, the same weekend I'd gone back home to fill my boots with Abby. It was Nicole, a tipsy, wobbly-eyed version, but Nicole nonetheless. He introduced her to me as 'the little lovely I told you about'. Donnie gets away with the odd sexist comment. He comes across as cute, harmless, a loveable larrikin, too smiley and twinkly of eye to be caught up in a web of boring old political correctness.

His talents in this field stem from his father, a thoroughbred cockney geezer who fashioned all the wink and patter necessary for survival in a tough place at a tough time. The East End was different back then. But Bob made it. The son of an Italian butcher, himself renowned for his handiwork with a meat cleaver, Bob Rossie rose swiftly to Robin Hood status. His name still heeds a reaction. A raised eyebrow, a knowing nod, a nervous rub of the temple. He is regarded with both reverence and fear, depending on your angle. When the bottom fell out of that world, when the cops began refusing backhanders and the whistleblowers started to sing like canaries, he scarpered pretty quick smart. Not to the Costa del Crime, the Algarve or Mexico but to Australia, where he continued to utilise his charm and his head for business, marrying a beautiful local who gave birth to a bouncing bambino called Donnie.

They call him Bombay Bob back home, so torn is he between the Old Country and the New World. He represents a healthy mix of 'wealth for toil' and 'God Save the Queen'; part bulldog, part pioneer. And, as the nickname suggests, he sits bang in the middle of the two nations. He owns a pub in Perth's northern suburbs called the Shakespeare Arms, which is chockfull of forty something ex-pats, swimming in a sea of Old

Spice and new money; the leather-skinned lasses with their orange faces and crows' feet smiles. Next to them their portly, polo-shirted partners, with their shiny red foreheads and damp denim shorts. Finally, their kids, sliding about on the postage stamp dance floor, in front of the Beatles cover band, Beckham and Owen emblazoned on their backs, unaware of the world their parents left behind, whole lives frozen, fossilized like shrines to the year they left Blighty.

The Shakespeare Arms is one big sweaty, sunburnt, pot-bellied, freckle-faced ex-pat embassy. It's a halfway house for visiting friends and a sheltered transit lounge for pale-faced newcomers, a quasi-quarantine that lasts for the rest of your stay, the rest of your life, if you like. It worked for us, and it works for Bob, a nice little earner, that's for sure. It lacks that waft of time, with all the creaks and scars that history brings, instead implying the passing of time through untreated wood and fake book spines. They're funny, those ex-pats. Most of them don't remember what a real English pub feels like. Moreover, they don't care. For them, England begins and ends with Basil Fawlty and Ian Botham. Anything after is unimportant, overshadowed by the big move, the beachside block and the fishing boat.

For every planeload that make it there's always a few who scuttle back, their shoulders burnt, pleading self-diagnosed acrophobia. They're the tails-between-the-legs brigade, the ping-pong Poms, back on the red-eye flight, skulking through Heathrow under cover of darkness, making a beeline for the nearest Marks and Spencer food hall and the latest episode of Coronation Street. Most never return, not to live anyway. It would never work. The kids would just whinge about the cold, the lack of space and all the old people walking slowly on purpose in the shopping centres and at the front of bus queues.

The northern subbies are Pommie paradise. Australia Light, Diet Australia, a watered down version of the real thing, of the country as a whole, with all the sand, sea and space you can swallow. You get the glorious beaches and the bloated residence without having to put up with the Melbourne mullets or the Sydney prices. The soccer's on at a decent hour and you're that bit nearer the old place, sitting serenely on the western edge, facing the other way, towards the Indian Ocean and the Old Country. You can get a house with a pool, a built-in barbecue and a neighbour from Yorkshire, all for the price of a rabbit hutch in West London. There's nostalgia - Cup Final day and Christmas time - but not much in the way of homesickness. No regrets, no worries. And Bob Rossi's the shining example, running the pub where they drink.

We went over last year, for the Rugby World Cup, and spent most evenings in the Shakey, watching games, getting drunk slowly. More Shakin' Stevens than Stratford playwright, it belies its tacky milieu. It's a place of celebration, a gathering of like minds and predictable pasts, a space to wallow in the dividends of your bravery. It sells all the beers you'd never drink back home, has tartan-clad, backpacker bar staff and a mock-marble bust of Billy S. sitting proudly on the edge of the public bar, just below the oversized plastic quill that sways gently in the cool puff of aircon.

Donnie came over to London to get in touch with the Englishman that lurked beneath. He was the bulldog puppy, desperate to have a feel of the old place before it

71

faded irretrievably from his blood. It was the call of the past. After all Bob's stories of the old place, of London's tough underworld with its gangsters, its community spirit, of nights around the piano, rolling out the barrel, trading banter and rhyming slang, Donnie had to see the place for himself, find out who he is, who his father is, who his father was. He enrolled at university in west London, settled into the student accommodation, met me, and introduced me to Nicole.

I was very glad he hadn't tried it on first, before I had the chance to lay some less flashy but ultimately quite effective groundwork. As he said her name, he winked at me - blatantly. It was possibly the most inappropriate wink in history, the candour of which left me blushing like a beacon for sad bastards everywhere. He then slithered off in search of the first team hockey captain, leaving me alone with Nicole. I just stood there, grinning without due cause. You see I get a little (a lot) nervous around beautiful (most) women, especially when I'm sober. Still, determined to make a fist of it, I pulled up a stool, watched her work and, between hefty gulps of lager, tried to look and sound stimulating. We chatted intermittently, each micro-conversation keeping me going until the next, each enforced gap working in my favour, giving me time to think, time to drink. And it seemed to work.

I remember one asinine discussion surrounding the gender of God. I don't recall how it began, but can summon it's contents like a transcript. Nicole asserted that God simply *had* to be a guy because he delegated childbirth to women. I said this couldn't be so as no male god in his right mind would put the genitals of his own gender on the outside of the body. She reluctantly agreed, admitting this was a definite design fault, especially as the only thing most boys prioritise above sex is football – an activity that leaves them vulnerable to all manner of woe. She suggested a better idea might have been to have them in a box and carry them around but I pointed out we'd just lose them sporadically, only to find them two days later down the back of the sofa, covered in fluff and crumbs, amongst all the loose change. This in turn would no doubt kill the moment, meaning we'd be getting even less than when they were stuck to us. I asked her why it was that girls always insist on having one of our crisps, despite the genuine offer of a whole packet. She lifted her shoulders in mock bafflement, refusing to accept my notion of ownership.

She looked fantastic. Her hair was Baywatch blonde, the remnants of a fun-in-the-sun summer tan still glowing through her skin. She was wearing a black halter neck top and leather pants. She looked like Buffy, without the baggage and the stake. She was cool, fusing trendy and girly with effortless grace, and something danced between us that night. I remember being transfixed by her eyes and the way they lowered bashfully, almost apologetically, as she realized how intense she was being. I loved that, a chink of shyness, the perfect imperfection. Her hair was stretched back tightly into a ponytail. I wondered what it would look like down, whether I'd ever see it being worn that way, whether I'd ever touch it.

I kept going, just waiting for a roadblock. But none came. And as I gained confidence, so I began to wonder if these sporadic mutterings were justification for a date. The inauspicious surrounds of our student bar - with its sticky floors, its plastic glasses, its crap band and the faraway hum of rolled tobacco - were hardly the forum for budding romance. Still, I figured it worth a try. So I adopted what is now my axiom for education: aim for the stars and land in the front paddock. In other words, start with the hot barmaid and hope you get a nibble before you reach the female bouncer with a spider tattoo on her neck. Luckily, Nicole said yes. We hit it off, hooked up and grew together.

After three hours of intermittent conversation I walked her back to her halls of residence and, with the promise of that date, received what still remains my favourite ever peck on the cheek. Then I turned and bound home, full of the time we'd shared. Before going to bed I wrote her number on two separate bits of paper, just in case I lost one. Then I went and knocked on Connor's door to leave one of the bits of paper in his room. I was clearly at that point of inebriation between dumb and useless. Then I returned to my room and slipped into slumber mode, a ridiculous grin no doubt emblazoned on my see-through face. And, looking back, it may well have been the euphoric smile of a man in love. The thought had never entered my mind at the time but I think something changed in me that night. A night that has helped define who I am today.

The morning after I felt a bit pathetic and gormless. Yet beneath the hazy thud stirred a buzz of excitement. I was smitten. It was a really odd thing. In just a few hours a total stranger had made me feel so comfortable that all that remained was an acute sense of discomfort. It wasn't the type of discomfort I feel when I have to wear a tie. It didn't irritate me. But it did worry me. It upset my balance, like I was being pulled in a different direction, not necessarily against my will, but slightly beyond my control.

The next week we went out for drinks and a boogie. And it wasn't long before she was donning the university scarf and watching me play rugby. She didn't really like rugby back then. She just liked me, which made it all the more gratifying. And for my part, I continued to watch her at work. There's a definite art to being a barmaid. And, apart from being a dedicated student, that's what she was back then. She was in no way a *bartender*. That doesn't do her justice. There was nothing remotely androgynous about her manner. Nicole was a natural: just enough throwaway chitchat, just enough skin and just enough time and proximity with each punter. As a couple, we lasted right through university - a notorious black spot for any relationship - without undue bother. And last year we treated ourselves to a month under the Aussie sun, warming our backs and lapping up the rugby, a game she's since grown to love. It was a time of great joy and intense hardship. When we came back I fell out with my father. Then I fell out with Nicole. Finally, there was only myself left to fall out with.

So I did that as well.

Ours was the most amicable split in romantic history. Looking back it was actually far too amicable. We'd reached a blind alley only to panic and run in different directions, and at different speeds. A greater force had displaced the passion and there was an empty space, a yawning hole, scooped out on behalf of natural law.

Nicole: 'We're going nowhere.'

Me: 'I know.'

Nicole: 'I think we've lost something.'

Me: 'Me too.'

Nicole: 'It's all been so complicated.'

Me: 'Yep.'

Nicole: 'After everything that's happened …'

Me: '*I know*, I know.'

Nicole: 'I think I need to be on my own. Just me again.'

Me: 'Yeah. We've become too reliant. It's all too much.'

Nicole: 'Too soon.'

Me: 'Definitely.'

Nicole: 'I still love you, you know.'

Me: 'Yeah. Me too.'

I'm surprised we didn't shake hands, thank each other for all the time and effort and promise to exchange Christmas cards. It was so matter-of-fact that the nearer we came to undoing everything the harder it was to halt the momentum. People talk about the importance of closure; we weren't so much closing the relationship as hanging the 'out to lunch' sign on it. If one of us had created the problem then we could have unravelled it, got to the source and hammered it out. As it was we were clueless, grasping at minor issues, creating struggle from nothing.

Life for us had, quite literally, stopped.

So with Nicole and I over, the boys took me out on the town. We tried every pub in West London but none of them provided a suitable answer. So we laid our communal self to rest in some seedy lap-dancing club. I staggered to the toilets and vomited my guts up, the suppressed thump of music and cheer ringing in my ears. Donnie wanted to drop me off at the knocking shop next door, urged me to screw my way out. But even in that state, the sputum dangling from my chin, the need to sink lower at the forefront of my mind, I drew back from the suggestion, choosing instead to stumble out the side door and crumple to a heap in the alleyway, eminently more comfortable in amongst the soft black bin bags, between the narrowest of walls.

They thought it was what I wanted. It wasn't. What I wanted was driving back to her parents' house in tears. I had neither the courage nor the know-how to turn things round. But I made a point of avoiding such places from then on in; the unconscious street corner pub, the cavernous brothel, the bookies, with its wall of smoke and slow rustle of debt, places where the air is thick with that unshakeable, noiseless angst, where men seep into the wallpaper, having nothing left of themselves. Instead I opted for the solitude of my room, not wishing to share my brittle turn of mood. A couple of days later Donnie came home to find me moping around the flat, playing sad songs and snivelling to myself.

He put his arm round me and said, 'Come on mate, less tears, more beers.'

I remember thinking at the time, is this really the answer, to desensitise myself? Is that what every man in history has done in my situation? If so, then no wonder we're all so messed up. No wonder women ridicule us for being emotional midgets. But I was too weak to make a stand.

I went out that night as well. I got drunk and ended up talking about Nicole. Given that day again, I wouldn't go out, I'd shed those tears and I'd listen to that music. And I'd talk *to* Nicole, not *about* Nicole. I was being dragged down by my own negativity, starting to believe I was surplus to her requirements; that I was acting like some sad bastard who couldn't release the truth. I hated the thought of being that person. Because I know what it did to my mother.

Nicole and I hadn't spoken for so long. I was determined the next time would be it. Make or break. Anything had to be better than not knowing. And I promised myself that next time I'd be ready, the words sitting impatiently on the tip of my tongue, handsome, charged, rehearsed.

But the next time was suddenly right now.

And I was miles from being prepared.

I was faltering, on one leg, half dressed, unready, in the change room of a department store, trying on jeans, my old ones lying in a crumpled heap on the floor, the new ones sitting round my ankles. I caught a glimpse of myself in the mirror. I kind of wished I hadn't. It's never a great look.

But it was definitely Nicole.

It was like a bedroom farce, Saturday afternoon TV, sport on all the other channels, one for the oldies, black and white, ever so English. I'd been caught with my trousers down and was about to be shoved into the wardrobe by a naughty, frisky housewife whose beefy, paranoid, jealous husband was due home any moment, while the elderly vicar finished his tea and cucumber sandwich in the front room.

I'd stopped breathing. After taking one colossal breath I'd become too frightened to exhale, in case, well, I'm not sure why, it just didn't seem right to breathe. What do I do, wait for her to go (and miss my chance), put on my old jeans and walk out (and say what) or put on the new ones, stroll out and use them as an icebreaker? I conducted a swift appearance check:

I'd had a shower, was clean-shaven, my hair had been cut recently and was waxed-up, my shirt was an acceptable former favourite and the denim jacket hanging on the wall was a personal triumph. Shame about the nose but there wasn't a great deal I could do about that given the restrictions of time and the lack of a plastic surgeon in the family. Besides, the good old sympathy vote should never be underestimated.

Okay, I'll go out, I thought, reaching for the curtain.

Then I stopped.

Better put trousers on first.

I was just about to go out again when I froze for the second time. What if she was with *him*, Toby the teacher? I don't think I could cope with seeing them together. What with last night, seeing Abby North again, and now this, it was starting to take its toll. So I went up to the curtain and looked through the gap. Until now it had always annoyed me that the curtains in these changing rooms didn't pull right across. I often felt exposed, like the whole world could see my bare arse. Sometimes I wondered if it was just a cunning sales ploy, if they were leeching off people's insecurities; guys everywhere walking around in ill fitting jeans, bought without trying on, the risk of flopping out in front of a shop full of strangers too much to bear.

But for once I was glad of the gap. I used it to my advantage, took a peak. I could see Donnie, Nicole's best friend Sara, and there she was - Nicole. I pulled back the curtain and went over. Just before I got to them one of the shop assistants stopped and asked me if the jeans were a good fit. Pre-occupied with my next move I replied with an indifference unbefitting the tension I felt within.

'I don't know. I didn't try them on.'

And with that I handed them over. The look she wore was not dissimilar to the one Connor received from the new barmaid at The Fox and Hounds after that gay thing. Then Nicole turned; she saw me, her mouth curling into a smile. I hadn't even considered the appropriate greeting: kiss-hello, firm but friendly handshake, formal nod, cool wink, fruity slap on the arse? Before I'd had the chance to select one Nicole walked the two steps towards me, pecked me on the cheek and we shared a brief, comfortable embrace.

'Hi Sam, how are you?'

'Good. How are you?

'I'm well, very well. It's nice to see you.'

'Yeah, you too.'

'Donnie was just telling us about Connor. What a nightmare. Are you okay?'

'Me? Yeah, bit of a sore nose.'

'I can see.'

'I'll be okay. It was poor old Connor who came out worse.'

'So I hear. Would it be okay to go and see him?'

'Of course, he'd like that.'

Time for action.

'Listen, are you guys doing anything now? Only we were planning on going for a drink and a bite to eat. Do you fancy coming along?'

'Yeah, cool. I'm in, Sara?'

'Too right, I've been dragged around the shops without proper sustenance for long enough. You boys have saved me. If I have to go to another boutique for skinny bitches, I'll scream.'

'Join the club,' said Donnie. 'I hate all the waiting outside the changing rooms, makes you feel like a bloody curb crawler or something.'

'I know, and then you get like three different shop assistants come up and ask you if you're okay, all with funny looks, and you're like, 'Of course I'm okay; just because I haven't got a shoehorn big enough for one of those Barbie doll dresses, I'm still okay. Hungry, but okay.'

'Yeah, nothing a Big Mac wouldn't sort out.'

Nicole and I looked at each other, knowingly. It was a reassuring exchange. We'd always shared a lot in common, Nicole and I, so much more than just time. There's the love of shopping, the same friends, the trip to Australia and let's not forget, for a time, we shared the expectancy of having a baby together.

Then we shared its loss.

Then we stopped sharing altogether.

11
Tuesday: 7:07am (eight months ago)

The scene at Heathrow Airport was a little strained. There were so many family members, so many good wishes and so many people making me promise to look after Nicole, I thought we'd never get to the duty free fags. I promised to do the right thing and at the time I truly meant it. In the end I didn't know whether I'd kept those promises or not.

We were only going to Australia for a month; anyone would think we were going off to war. In a way I guess we were, being fully paid-up members of the Barmy Army.

Sitting in the boarding lounge, we breathed in the expectancy of it all. Twenty hours between us, Donnie, Jonny Wilkinson and a free tab at the Shakespeare Arms. We'd saved our money, bought our tickets and shopped for spring. It was time to clutch hands and smile at the thought of a month away together on the other side of the world. It would include both the best and worst times of our lives. Still, given the chance, I'd go again. I'd go in a heartbeat.

We were on our way to Perth, Western Australia. We had both taken a mix of accrued and unpaid leave, our bosses mutually unhappy but who cared, that's what relief teachers are for. Nicole felt bad about neglecting her students for so long whilst I was only too glad to leave the little buggers back at the zoo for a while, wiping their own arses.

We snuggled up on the plane and watched London shrink into the distance. The clouds fizzed in and out of view and soon we were higher than we'd ever been. Every so often Nicole would grip my hand, giving it a short, tight squeeze. We watched the big electronic map on the screen in front of us, plotting our journey over Eastern Europe, looking for Georgia for no other reason than we'd be seeing them get clobbered by England in a matter of days, live. The Army were in full voice, a somewhat limited set list being belted out with admirable gusto. For the first six hours, at least. After that the rigours of long haul flying took their toll, reducing the in-flight singsong to the odd slurry burst from the back row. The crew breathed a collective sigh of relief; safe in the knowledge it'd be a couple of hours between offers to join the mile high club. It was sad to see and hear them fade, like part of the holiday was already over. Fatigue began to take charge; flags sunk impotently, war paint smudged from red and white to fuzzy pink, faces told stories of too much booze and not enough forethought. The toddlers on the third row were the most upset, confused as to why the funny man in front had stopped making faces and belching the national anthem. Interspersed amongst the snoring soldiers of war sat clusters of puzzled, baggy-eyed civilians, each wondering why they'd been forced to spend a whole day of their lives between an alcoholic broker called Rupert and a psychopathic soccer thug named Wayne. It was World Cup time, and not even England's meticulously erected class barriers were safe from toppling under the heavy weight of sporting fervour.

My excitement had been tempered slightly by the news that Donnie was carrying an extra wheel. He'd gone over a few days before to meet up with this American backpacker he'd stumbled upon in a bar in Covent Garden the month before. This is what he does, or at least did – meet extraordinarily good-looking women and bonk them, without any regard for his friends. It was outrageous. This was *our* holiday, not the property of some gooey-eyed yank with no concept of the magnitude of the occasion. She'd be the one with the pigtails, the college sweater and the pom-poms, her all-American jaw line chomping on gum, bouncing on the spot, overbearingly nice, banging on about how psyched she is to be here for the World Series Rugby Grand Finals.

What does a mate really get out of that sort of situation? Yes, she'll no doubt be decent eye candy but I've never been one for lecherous ogling at my friend's partners. Not when my girlfriend was so superior. I guess I may, in time, by some stroke of cosmic genius, learn to enjoy her company but, let's face it, the negative repercussions for close friends far outweigh the positives. He changes, we change, we see less of him, we never see him on his own and when we do see him the conversation is a timid, diluted shadow of its former self; a pre-watershed debacle that could only be resuscitated by her swift departure. Nothing personal, it's just life and love, the collision of your two favourite things. But therein lies the crux; they're *his* two favourite things. Not mine.

It was always different with Nicole, though.

She was meant to be long-term.

Once the last rendition of *Swing Low, Sweet Chariot* had died a slow death Nicole and I drifted into a dreamy sleep together. There was one last feeble stab at my personal favourite - the witty, wordy 'Oh Jonny, Jonny, Jonny, Jonny, Jonny, Jonny Wilkinson' - from a fat bloke in the toilet, but it seemed nothing in the world could come between us, certainly not a planeload of rowdy rugger buggers or even a gate-crashing floozy from Utah.

But something did come between us.

And it was cruel irony.

The one thing that stopped us growing, that made us question our strength and compatibility, was the one thing produced by our love.

Our baby.

We were only a week into the holiday when Nicole told me she was pregnant. She'd suspected for a couple of days and had taken the test one morning while I was still asleep. At the time we were on a trip down the west coast, hugging the Indian Ocean. We'd seen England beat the plucky Georgians and were gearing up for the big showdown with South Africa on the Saturday. These were the only two games we were going to see live, for the rest of the trip we'd have to make do with the giant screen in the Shakey. Donnie had met us alone. He'd dumped the poor American traveller on account of the fact she kept hassling him about spending too much time in his old man's boozer and neglecting his day-tripping duties. Typical Donnie, can't meet them halfway.

We woke early and headed for the jetty on our way to a dolphin cruise. It was the perfect morning, clear and warm with the promise of a full day's spring sunshine. The nearest cloud must have been a lifetime away. I certainly couldn't see it coming as the boat cruised smoothly into gear. There was a hint of cool in the summer breeze, reminding us how early it was, and how hot it would be later. You could see for miles. I stared in awe as we cut through the vast blue blanket of ocean in front, giving us ample space to breathe and ponder. The dolphins danced, cruised and leapt beside the boat. Every so often one would twirl around and swim belly-up at the front, showing beauty and childishness in equal measure. Others were less animated, keeping their distance. They were the ones protecting their young.

That evening we strolled along the stretch of beach near our hotel. I remember thinking the sand there was darker than on the city beaches. I loved the beaches back in Perth, with their perfect white sand, their volleyball courts, their lifeguards and beautiful people. But there was something about the ruggedness of these less fashionable beaches that stirred me. They were untamed, untouched, cultivated by a world of time, with an almost arrogant disregard for the precious and precarious nature of human life. The great thing about a beach like that is it engages all your senses. You feel the sand, smell the air, see the beauty and taste the salt. And when your senses combine it makes you think, think about things you wouldn't normally think about. You contemplate, imagine and reminisce at the beach. That's why we flock there whenever we can. That's why

Australians are lucky; you can find a beach and have it all to yourself, for hours at a time, just for you. Great for kids, for friends and for lovers, and a great place to be told you're going to be a dad.

If you're ready for the news, that is.

We strolled along. Then Nicole started talking about those dolphins and their calves. Looking back now I can see what she was getting at, at the time it was all a bit subtle, flying straight over my head and into the ocean. She was talking about how the dolphins that swam with their young didn't seem to be having as much fun as the others, how they seemed very content in their own way. I just presumed she was getting caught up in the moment or that she'd had one too many glasses of the local wine at dinner. Then I realised she'd been drinking soft drinks for the last couple of days, ever since Sunday's match, yet I still didn't pick the clues. She soon realised I wasn't nibbling at her bait and just came out with it.

'We're having a baby.'

'Bullshit.'

I know. It was a ridiculous thing to say. I'm not very good in those situations, those times that call for an intensely profound or witty comment, to be remembered forever, brought up at dinner parties and family gatherings. I'm no good off the cuff, especially when I'm confronted with life-altering news. I wish I'd said something cool and romantic like 'just when I think you can't possibly make me any happier …' Still, what I said made her laugh and, after a while, you don't really mind if they're laughing with you or at you, as long as they're happy. And she was. I just couldn't see it, I couldn't see past my own sensibilities.

We hugged and said how great it was and how we'd get through it together and all that sort of stuff. But I didn't sound very convincing. I knew I didn't. I didn't really want to. There was a large part of me that wanted Nicole to know how scared I was at the thought of fathering a child. I couldn't help it. We carried on walking along the beach, but instead of doing so together I fell behind Nicole's step. It wasn't far but the gap was significant. I was already out of sync with her. And there was this song lyric I couldn't get rid of, from a *Counting Crow's* track we'd listened to a hundred times before, one of my all-time favourites, one of our favourites. They were our words, yet suddenly, without warning those words turned against us.

She walks along the edge of where the ocean meets the land.

Just like she's walking, on a wire, in the circus.

My life was now out of my control; things were about to spiral away from the place I'd created, meticulously. There were no shocks there, no dangers, no twists. There was suddenly no in-between; it was all or nothing, right or wrong; and I didn't feel anywhere near ready to be reliant on fate and health and hope and life itself in order to stay happy. It would either be perfect or disastrous. Suddenly the sea felt cold and the sand gritty. I gathered myself and caught up with Nicole. She turned and smiled but it was all too late. I'd already fallen too far back.

Things weren't meant to happen that way; it wasn't the right order or time. Nicole knew I'd react like this. She knew how hurt and confused I'd been by my parents divorce. She knew how insecure I was about the responsibility of children. I didn't know if I was capable of being a good father. I didn't know if I was cut out for it. It wasn't as if I'd had a particularly good role model. We were meant to be travelling, free and easy, creating memories we could one day haul out and share with our children. For the next couple of days my mind raced and I wasn't there for Nicole. I was happy the way we were. We were off work, in Australia, with friends, watching England, going to the Shakey, enjoying a free bar.

Most people get the best part of nine months to adjust but I was judged on my initial reaction. I never got the opportunity to work through my anxieties and come out the other end. I never got the chance to grow into a parent. It wasn't actually that long before I came round. But it may as well have been a lifetime. None of it would have mattered if we'd had the baby, it all would have been forgotten, laughed off, typical bloke and all that. But we didn't have the baby and it wasn't forgotten; it was dragged up and thrown back at me.

I was coming round, fast. At the South Africa game, under a week after being told on the beach, I remember thinking that my kid was there, with us, when Jonny tore them apart in the second half. The rock steady drop goals, the roar of the Army, the banter on the train from Subiaco to Joondalup, the party in the Shakey afterwards, he was there too. I didn't say it though, it sounded tacky, fuelled by booze, highly inappropriate, like I hadn't quite grasped the concept yet, the magnitude of the situation. It's true, I hadn't. But I was getting there. And by the time of the miscarriage I was all the way there, and Nicole knew it. She just preferred to bring up the other stuff, it was easier, quicker, less complicated.

They say the first twelve weeks are the critical time. If you can get through them you're pretty much home and dry. We lost the baby when Nicole was twenty-one weeks pregnant, freakishly late by all accounts. Twenty weeks. That's five months, nearly half a year. A long time whichever way you look at it. A lifetime.

She was showing. I could see and feel our baby. We'd just had the twenty-week scan and everything was okay. We were back in England, getting ready for a night out. I'd booked a table at this flash restaurant up west, recommended by Donnie. I wanted it to be special. Nicole had been in the bathroom for ages when I realised I couldn't hear her. I knocked on the door and asked if she was okay. There was no answer. I asked again and there was still no sign. Knowing she'd been feeling particularly unwell of late, I barged the door open with my shoulder, to find her lying on the floor, lifeless save for a sluggish puddle of deep red blood that was loitering, threatening my whole world. I ran over to her and bent down. She was quivering slightly and she was crying.

'I'm scared Sam,' she whispered, 'I'm so scared.'

In my pocket was a small velvet box with a ring inside. I was planning to ask Nicole to marry me that night, not because she was pregnant but because she was special. But the moment passed by and as much as I tried to get it back, it never returned. I had high hopes for that ring, now it sits, unused, bogged down at the bottom of my sock draw. I rushed Nicole to hospital and, after a long and anxious wait, they said she was going to be okay, despite the miscarriage. But I knew she wouldn't be okay, not really.

She left hospital with an empty womb and empty arms. I told her she was doing fine when we all knew she wasn't. She wasn't meant to be, that was the point. I read all the leaflets. I knew that miscarriages occur because of chromosomal abnormalities or structural defects in the embryo. I knew the foetal loss rate for somebody that far gone is less than three percent. And I knew that some couples experience relationship difficulties during this time. I knew this only too well. And I also knew that our baby was at a stage where it could hear its mother's voice and her heartbeat. Our baby was fully developed.

And I knew our baby was a boy. Our son.

I wasn't dealing with it all that well myself, but by trying to be positive for Nicole, I was sounding like I just wanted to move on. But I didn't, not really. I wanted to deal with that horrible, empty loss. I just didn't know where to start. And seeing Connor half-dead on the pavement had brought all the memories flooding back. It wasn't just the sight of a loved one cut down, inert, a frozen heap smothered in blood, or the smell of hospitals and the waiting, or the overwhelming feeling of helplessness, that took me back there. Most of all it was that gut-wrenching realisation that things would never be the same again.

12
Sunday, 1:09 pm

Seeing Nicole again had definitely lifted my mood. There was a warmish flicker, a deep-seated glow, and although it quivered relatively dimly, it was far from being blown out.

She looked great too. She was wearing an Adidas tracksuit top, old school, tight, in powder blue; three-quarter-length beige cargo pants, and a pair of dainty white Reeboks. As we walked towards one of the pubs by the river I couldn't help notice the number of male rubberneckers having a good perv at her as she moved beside me. It unsettled me, but I kept my nerve and got on with the job of lifting myself beyond the rabble.

We sat out in a beer garden overlooking the steady journey of the Thames. The air was sharp but the fragile sun was doing its best to lift the chill. We decided to sit outside until our food was ready. I felt a bit nervous at the thought of eating in front of Nicole. I know that sounds silly, I'd eaten in front of her a million times before. Nevertheless I purposely chose something that wasn't going to make me dribble, squirt, spit, slurp, smell or look like a slob - a toasted ham and cheese sandwich. Nicole ordered a ham and salad baguette (I hoped for the same reason.) If she'd have gone for the spaghetti bolognaise with extra garlic I would have felt deflated. Donnie, for the record, had a burger with the lot, which shows how conscious he is of eating in front of the opposite sex. He told us that Amber the model loved up-market restaurants where a cropped lettuce leaf and a baby tomato constitute a whole meal. He admitted that whenever he went out to dinner with her these days he had a bacon sandwich before he left. It had turned into a bizarre gastronomic good luck charm.

It was just like old times and I didn't want it to end. I wanted us to spend the whole day together, to walk along the river, get a couple of hot chocolates and sit on the grass watching the boats, her head on my shoulder. But we were miles away from the old days and as we all got up to leave, I began to feel empty. We said our goodbyes and the transient happiness slipped away.

'It's been cool, Sam. Can I call you?'

It may have been nothing, it may have been a palpitation brought on by high blood pressure, but my heart undeniably lifted.

'Yeah, of course; that would be really good.' My reply was swift and patently keen. She hardly had time to complete her question. I was no good at acting cool.

As Donnie and I got back in the car he looked over to me and said, 'What are you two playing at? You're made for each other.'

I smiled back and said, 'I know.'

'Hell of a coincidence, bumping into her like that,' he added.

'You called her, didn't you?'

'Who me?' he replied, cheesy grin and all.

We went home and both fell asleep, Donnie in front of the rugby, me on my bed. The stress and strain of the last twenty-four hours - not to mention the two pints at lunchtime - had all taken its toll. Later we went up to the hospital to see Connor. I thought he still seemed overly chirpy but was willing to give him the benefit of the doubt. When we got back home I rang Kathy - Connor's boss and potential love match - and told her the whole story. She started crying and said she'd go straight up to see him. I said I'd look after Chloe, her five-year-old daughter, as seeing Connor in that state might scare her. Granted, she had a bit of emotional baggage, but Kathy had the hots for Connor, big time. And he fancied her too, but they'd never quite got it together. She'd separated from her ex-husband and was back on the market and ready to go. Only cupid's arrow was stuck in the arse of a man - namely Connor - who rarely flew by the seat of his pants, whose usual tactic was to bore women into sleeping with him.

Chloe wasn't the issue. She loves Connor, mainly because he's an immature oaf and kids appreciate that quality in an adult. It gives them hope for the future. And those feelings were reciprocated. Donnie and I were convinced that they'd make a great couple. But then again, the sum of what Donnie and I knew about successful long-term relationships could be written on the back of a postage stamp. No, the problem was that Connor's the type of guy who laughs in the face of spontaneity. For him, impulsiveness is the enemy. He worships at the altar of prudence and, when pushed on the issue, always states that he will go for it in his own time, in his own way, when he's good and ready and not a moment before, even if there's another Ice Age between drinks. Stability personified is Connor. He's as stubborn as an adolescent mule and has an arms-folded single-mindedness that can leave you frustrated to the point of violence. They've had the odd random snog but nothing concrete. He's probably on stage two of a meticulous master plan. He's done it before.

There was this girl at university called Petra who, in spite of having the name of a German Shepherd dog and the conversational skills of an anti-social monk, Connor liked. He really liked her. He admired this pretty but shy girl from the distance of a lecture theatre for six long months before finally plucking up the courage to ask her out. And he kept to this stringent plan, with caution as its backbone, a plan of attack drawn up using military precision previously unseen outside the walls of NASA. First he introduced himself, by asking if he could borrow a pen. And that was it for a couple of weeks. He re-grouped and stalled. Then he suggested a textbook before worming his way into her discussion group. The word 'discussion' should be used with caution. Petra didn't say much. Indeed, Connor would get quite hot under the collar if eye contact were made; as for nervous smiles and nods of recognition, that was the stuff of dreams. The plan trundled along, not so much the blind leading the blind as the tentative leading the over-cautious. After three long months they were involved in a joint project together. If the two of them had been projected live on a bizarre reality TV show it would have been like visual water torture for an entire nation.

Drip. She said she likes reading. Drip. He said he likes reading too. Drip. She likes movies. Drip. Him too. Drip. That's why she's doing Film Studies. Drip. Him too. Drip. Amazing Coincidence. Drip. Yeah. Drip. Isn't it just? Drip. Aren't those two a pair of? Drips.

When Connor finally asked Petra if she'd like to go for a drink she said okay. The plan had actually worked. Operation Tedium was a success. She said yes, or at least she would have said yes had she been staying at university and not moving back home to Scotland at the weekend. Apparently Petra was a bit unhappy in London because she didn't seem to be making any friends. Funny that. It was a cruel blow, a hapless tale of the perils of over-caution. Connor's my best mate in the whole world but sometimes he can't half be a ... *Drip.*

This episode only seemed to heighten Connor's fear of change, of extending himself, of flirting with possibility instead of relying on probability. Once ensconced in a job that interested him slightly he set up camp and pulled the shutters down. Then, by the time he'd realised it wasn't what he really wanted; it was too late. And suddenly he was unhappy. He felt trapped. He didn't mind working in the video store. He quite liked being surrounded by movies, after all his degree was in Film Studies. But he rightly feels that it should have led to more than a job with a badge that said, 'Hi, I'm Connor – I can help!'

And he hated the owner, Nigel. I couldn't blame him for that. The bloke is a sad case; a greasy-fringed jobsworth who patronizes Connor and drools over Kathy. And if it weren't for the fact he liked working with Kath and watching movies (and paying his rent) then Connor would have told Nigel the video nasty where to shove his job a long time ago.

It was never part of his life's ambition to work as an assistant in *Movieland*. And it certainly didn't help that the owner was a weasel and the assistant manager a figure of unrequited love. Having said that, it was never part of his plan to move from Ireland to England or to lose his father to cancer a few weeks before his twelfth birthday. Connor's both incredibly intelligent and somewhat unambitious to boot. It's a worrying combination and a slightly cruel hand to be dealt. He's your classic academic; head always buried in a book or engrossed in some documentary; yet the bright lights of the world outside had him turning away, squinting at the sheer banality of it all.

I'm sure Connor would love a slice of Donnie's verve, his lack of compunction, his unerring belief that the glass is half full and on the verge of a top-up. Their respect is mutual, with me somewhere in between. Donnie loves Connor's wit, envies his mind. Connor wishes he could talk to the girls like Donnie, or enjoy a special relationship with his father like Donnie does. We'd both like his monthly pay cheque; his chiselled Mediterranean features and his buffed physique. I'm really looking forward to the day he finally bellyflops into that Italian gene pool, with its reverse cycle metabolism. And I'm sure Donnie would have liked a crack at Nicole, instead of leaving her for me. Not too many birds that tasty get past our Don. He used to look at her funny, at the start. I never mentioned it for fear he'd suddenly snap, realizing he should in fact have a go, shoulder barging me out the way. I'd catch him, not perving as such, just looking, intensely.

There's always been balance. At uni, Donnie was captain of the firsts while I sat comfortably in the seconds. As for Connor, he was chuffed to get a run out in the thirds, or 'turds' as they were fondly referred to.

Donnie was one of those lightning left-wingers, always ending up with a hat trick of tries and a clean kit. I was the nuggetty scrum half; linking the donkey forward pack and the pretty-boy back line. I delivered a good, reliable pass but was lacking in real bulk or pace. Then there was Connor, second rower, obligatory knee strapping and headband, demon catch in the line-out but a bit heavy-legged round the paddock, usually about three phases behind the play. We'd play our respective matches before meeting up with Nicole and the others in the bar afterwards, to trade war stories, bend the truth a little. More often than not, we'd end up in some curry house somewhere, our university ties around our heads, more lager down our shirts than in our glasses.

In second year, when we first got the flat, we'd stay up late drinking tinnies, the three of us, watching *Goodfellas* on video. Connor would spout off all manner of shit about wide angles and close-ups, while Donnie and I role-played the fight scenes. Then Connor would suddenly get up, reeling off reams of perfectly recounted dialogue. We'd just sit there, engrossed, in awe, looking forward to the day we saw his name on the big screen.

I feel proud the two of them met through me. There was a time I felt like I was in the middle, hovering precariously between my old and new lives, between the scholar and the stud. But the two of them soon clicked, then grew; now the lines are so blurred I'm not sure where one part stopped and the other one started. I guess it doesn't matter.

Kathy dropped Chloe off and the two of us spent the next couple of hours watching one of the cartoon channels on cable. I tried to explain how the old cartoons are better than the ones of today but Chloe wasn't having any of it. We watched *Scooby-Doo* to exemplify my point. I couldn't believe that, firstly, Chloe didn't agree that it was far superior to those tiresome *Rugrats* and, secondly, that Shaggy was the spitting image of Connor. She became quite hot under the collar, saying that Uncle Connor was much nicer, lovelier and prettier than the other skinny ginger man. I thought about drumming home all the palpable physical similarities – like the fact neither of them owned an arse, just a hole at the bottom of their respective backs – but was fearful of the reprisals.

Sitting there with Chloe I couldn't help but wonder what life would've been like if we'd had the baby, how cool it would be if I were sitting there with my son, chatting away, watching TV, being called Daddy. And every so often I checked that the phone was still working.

Just in case.

13
Monday: 10:22 am

We set off for the hospital again around mid-morning the next day. Connor had discharged himself, adding to the general swell of concern. So Donnie and I both chucked sickies in order to welcome him home, and sound him out.

Donnie works in the city where, so I believe, time is money. But, to his credit, he was determined to be there for Connor. For me it was just a question of phoning through lesson plans I hadn't actually done and pointing out which kids would be providing hotspots for an unsuspecting relief teacher.

We were both looking forward to having him home, although were sure he'd milk the situation dry, malingering for a couple of years before showing any genuine signs of recovery. We were convinced, for example, that on our arrival he'd still be in his pyjamas, or at best, sickly-looking leisurewear, waiting for assistance with his bags, excuses for his apathy ranging from post-traumatic stress to bed sores. Put it this way, we were prepared for more than a modicum of bone idleness. Still, we figured that was okay, for a while at least. We'd missed the whingeing git, despite being disinclined to ever mention it to him. What we weren't prepared for was what we actually saw. On arrival Connor was sitting in the television lounge, showered, spruced, fully dressed in clothes none of which remotely resembled a pair of grey towelling tracksuit pants, bags packed and stored neatly beside him, watching *Jerry Springer*.

'How's it going boys, all ready for the off? I'll just finish this brew and I'll be right with you.'

He was holding up a white plastic cup that presumably contained tea. He had only been in hospital for a couple of days but was already a lot more coherent. The swelling had eased and he had a bit more colour. He got out of his chair and Donnie grabbed him, arms outstretched, like a mafia boss, like a Don, all gel and labels and gold, head to one side. It always felt good with Donnie; he knew how to hold another man. It's the Italian in him, and the gangster.

He held Connor at arm's length, in control, his bony brown hands with their tufts of black hair, gripping tight on his shoulders. He held Connor's face, palms cupped, gently tapping his cheeks, as if he was about to smack a sloppy one on him, right on the lips. Fortunately Donnie's only half Italian and baulks at kissing men.

'We've come to take you home, big man.'

'Bring it on.'

'How you feeling today, Con?' I asked.

He heard me but did not answer, instead asking one of his own. 'Do you know who the real genius is behind the Jerry Springer Show?'

'I wasn't aware there were any,' I said, trying to inject some much-needed cynicism into proceedings, still reeling from his blatant disregard for my question.

'I know,' said Donnie, already loving the direction of the conversation. 'The true genius is the dude who does the bleeping out. That's a full-time job right there. Oh, and that bald security guy, hats off to him; he has to break up scraps between flabby chicks and their trailer trash mullet-dude boyfriends. Yep, I'll go with the bald security guy or the bleep dude.'

It never ceases to amaze me how deeply Donnie and Connor get involved in the most trivial of subjects. This one sounded like it could drag on for a while so I pulled up a chair and picked up a two-year-old copy of *Women's Weekly* from the coffee table in front of the TV. I was hoping to find an article entitled, *'Getting back together - the way to your ex's heart'* or something along those lines, a secret portal to the other world. As it was I was drawn towards a piece entitled, *'Your son is gay, what should you say?'* Underneath was an eight-point checklist of things to do and say when your son outs himself in front of you. I soon realised that despite the lack of an eight-point checklist my mother had scored fairly highly. As far as I was aware she didn't provide him with any relevant phone lines or literature but did encourage him to talk candidly, making all the right noises as regards pride and guilt and self worth. My father didn't do too badly either. At least he *tried* to hide his feelings of confusion and disappointment – which was number seven.

'All good points, Donnie,' continued Connor. 'But you're wrong on both counts, my friend.'

'Bugger, thought I had that one in the bag, Con,' he replied, genuinely peeved.

'The real genius behind the *Jerry Springer Show* is the guy who comes up with the show titles. Every single one is about the same thing, yet he keeps churning out new and interesting titles: 'Love Triangles', 'Threesomes', 'I'm shagging around', 'I'm sleeping with two people', 'I'm screwing a bird *and* a geezer', 'I'm fucking every fucker'. You've got to hand it to him; he's a very talented guy. Am I right or am I fucking right?'

'Fair comment, well argued.'

With Donnie suitably impressed, Jerry started his final thought. So we all got up and headed for the lift. No one watches that bit. The show's about making normal people feel better about their lives; we're not in it for the moral guidance, especially from a bloke that had just completed a show entitled, *'We're not getting wed, there's someone else in my bed'*. Connor seemed to be moving okay. And he insisted on carrying his own bags, waving and winking at a couple of nurses on the way out. As the automatic doors swished closed behind us, I stopped and wondered if I'd ever visit this hospital for a good reason.

One of Connor's bags was a blue plastic one that carried all the magazines and books he'd been reading whilst in hospital. 'You could open your own newsagents with all that gear, Con,' I suggested, exaggerating the weight of the bag in mock-pain.

'Ha, I've got bigger fish to fry than that, Sammy-boy.'

Now it was nothing unusual to hear Connor being cryptic, he was famous for it. But that last comment worried me. It worried me because it implied a certain amount of ambition, which, with all due respect to Connor, wasn't altogether normal. Especially when one considers the blind optimism and total lack of recognition for what had been an incredibly traumatic incident. Maybe I was being paranoid or maybe Connor was just putting on a brave face. Either way it didn't seem right. Despite all of this, I let the comment slide, for the time being least.

'What are we doing now then boys?'

Connor was sat bolt upright in the passenger seat of Donnie's car, rubbing his hands with what can only be described as glee.

'Thought you'd want to get home and unpack, chill out a bit,' I said, trying desperately to reel him in.

His response was predictable.

'Then you thought wrong, Sam. Let's do something. I can sleep when I'm dead.'

'Well, I'm not drinking. It's too bloody dangerous,' insisted Donnie, picking up on my thread, trying to grab the reins himself.

'No, I don't want to *drink*,' said Connor. 'I'm still on painkillers, remember? Anyway, it's a bit sad that our first thought is to abuse our bodies with the evils of alcohol. We should be treating our bodies like temples, not trash cans.

Now I was frantic with worry.

'No,' he continued, 'I've got a much better idea. Let's go for a fry-up. Hospital food's shite.'

Phew.

I'd clearly strayed way off target with the old pocketbook psychology. This *was* the old Connor, full of crap but highly enjoyable to boot. And with that we checred. We cheered both Connor's sensible proposal as well as his welcome return to normality, and we headed straight for the sanctuary of our local café. We ordered our fry-ups, sat down on the sturdy pine chairs, opened the morning papers and slurped on our mugs of hot, sweet tea.

Then, like the proverbial dog with a bone, I attempted to get a straight answer from Connor. 'So, tell us, how *are* you feeling?'

It was a simple question, impossible to ignore, easy to answer. A question that would hopefully be the springboard to an important conversation, to a heartfelt exchange. It would clear the emotional clouds that hovered overhead, leaving a rounded composure more befitting our time-soaked bond.

'I fucking hate students.'

Here we go again.

'What?'

I was wound up now, truly sprung.

This sudden bout of aggression had come only moments after a fit of boundless euphoria. The Connor I know doesn't hate anyone, least of all students.

'What was that about students?' said Donnie, clearly as baffled as me.

'Well, get a load of that lot over there.'

Connor was pointing unashamedly at a group of five people sitting in the corner of the café, minding their own business.

'How do you know they're students?' I asked, immediately regretting the fact that I'd perpetuated the lunacy.

'It's obvious, innit? For a start, there's about ten of them, all huddled round a single plate of chips. Plus it's the middle of the day and they've got nothing better to do. And that one's got poor man's dreadlocks, and that one's wearing a *Radiohead* T-shirt, and they all smell. Shall I go on?'

He was talking at full volume, embarrassing himself. I wanted him to pull his head in, but couldn't help disputing his nonsense, this unhealthy fixation that was so obviously the support act for some bigger outfit; something we had to endure in order to arrive at the main event, the reason for coming.

'That's a bit hypocritical, don't you think? It wasn't that long ago *we* were all students, and we spent a fair bit of time in here as I recall.'

I wanted the argument. I felt like we needed it.

'We weren't like them though. They're rolling their own cigarettes and sharing them round. Have they no pride? A bloody good bath wouldn't go amiss either.'

'Come on, Con, what's up? It's time to spill your guts.'

'What … again?'

'You know what I mean.'

'Well, I've been doing a bit of thinking, that's all, Sam. There was a time, not so long ago, when I would have been jealous of those guys.'

'Jealous?'

'Of their lifestyle.'

'But not anymore?'

'No, that's the thing. I loved uni, it was the best time, but I loved it so much I haven't moved on since. I haven't got on with my life, not in the same way as you two, anyway. I had a lot of time to think in hospital. I'll be honest with you, I felt low, *really* low. But I took a long hard look at myself and figured out what it is I really want. My life's a joke compared to you two. I even sound like a joke, the one about the Englishman, the Australian *and the Irishman*. You know the rest. But not anymore, I plan to sort it out. It's time to snap out of

106

it and do something useful, exciting even, get some pride back, you know.'

'Any idea what?'

'Kind of.'

'What does that mean?'

'Well, I'm not going to skivvy for that little fucking Hitler in the video store anymore, that's for sure.'

'But you love movies.'

'It's all fantasy, Sam. I want to do it for real, live a little you know, have a pukka job, proper wedge, nice clobber, quality motor, maybe a decent piece of skirt, who knows.'

'Have you thought about learning to speak English first?'

This was Donnie.

'Keep up, Skippy, you've been in the big smoke long enough now. You know the score, my son.'

'Have you thought about *how*?'

'I've got plans.'

'That's good.'

'There's no time to dwell. I don't want to be one of those people who wear self-pity like a badge of honour. I don't want to amble through life anymore. This has been a wake-up call for me. I'm going to take some positives. Which reminds me, you'll never guess who visited me in hospital.'

'Kathy?' said Donnie.

'She did, yes, and it was really good to see her; I like her. I really like her. And that's something else I want to get sorted. But that's not who I'm talking about.'

'Nicole?'

'No, it's not her either, although she did visit me. She's a smashing girl, Sam. I hope you two can sort yourselves out, you were made for each other.'

Donnie looked at me, smiled, but said nothing.

'I'm not talking about her either,' Connor continued. 'By the way, did you two have a hidden fucking camera in there or something?'

'We give up,' I said, presuming Donnie had also had enough of this game.

'Terry Jones.'

'*Techno* Terry, from university?'

'The very same.'

'How is he?'

'Fantastic.'

'How did he know you were in hospital?'

'I'm not sure really, he heard it from someone.'

'Wow, good old Techno,' said Donnie. He heard the name and immediately got excited. Techno Terry has that effect on people.

'What's he up to these days? I haven't seen him in ages.'

'He's landed on his feet, big time. He was wearing this flash suit; driving around in this classy motor; earning some serious dough by all accounts. It was so good to see him. He gave me some hope. And he said there might be an opening in his firm for me. That's why I discharged myself. Techno's well up the ladder, might be able to sort me out. How good is that?'

'It's not dodgy, is it? After all, he was partial to a bit of drug dealing at uni. He was well into the old disco biscuits, as I recall.'

I hated to go on like an old fart but I wanted to make sure it was all above board. It wasn't subtle but Terry was renowned for his crooked deals, hot gear, moody money, iffy friends, you name it, he was always flirting with authority.

'No way, man. It's all kosher. Besides, he was hardly a drug dealer, just supplied a few of his mates, you included, if I'm not much mistaken. He's a sales rep for some big pharmaceutical firm.'

'Still into his chemicals, then?' I grunted, rather unhelpfully, it has to be said.

'It's not bent or anything. All legitimate. And I wouldn't mind a piece of the action myself, not to mention a bit of support from my so-called *mates*. Besides, you've got to be a graduate to work there so, finally, I'll be able to put my degree to some use.'

'Sounds awesome, Con; good on yer mate, we're *both* very pleased for you, aren't we Sam?' Donnie scowled across the table at me. I got the message.

'Yes, course we are. Look, I'm sorry Con, I didn't mean to doubt you. I just worry, that's all. You've been through a lot lately.'

'It's okay, Sam. Just goes to show what a laughing stock I've become if people start suspecting foul play when I mention I might be getting a job in *Sales*.'

'No, that's not true.'

I'd hurt his feelings. It had been a long few days and our collective fuse was a bit short. Luckily, Connor let it pass.

'It doesn't matter, Sam. Besides, I might not even get it. I've got an interview this afternoon and don't exactly look the part, do I? I mean, I can hardly speak, I'm walking with a limp and my ribs ache with every breath. Not exactly fighting fit.'

'Has Terry told them about the fight?' asked Donnie.

'Yeah, they know I'm not looking my best but apparently they're desperate for new reps. The company's expanding all the time. Hopefully I'll get the old sympathy vote. Techno Terry said he'd butter them up, sing my praises a bit.'

Our food arrived so we tucked in. There's nothing like a few strips of streaky, a couple of fat sausages, a dollop of scrambled and a fried slice to sort you out after a weekend like that. It was strange being back in the café on a weekday. Just like old times, only nothing like them, too. As I say, it was strange. We ended up having three mugs of tea whilst talking about Techno Terry and all the other people from college, all the people we'd promised to keep in touch with but, for one reason or another, never did.

Techno Terry was certainly high on that list, especially for Connor. Permanently chirpy, an overgrown schoolboy, he and Connor got pretty tight at uni. They both studied film and media, Connor always helping Techno out with essays and presentations. Now, against all the odds, Terry was returning the favour.

Techno Terry was forever on the verge of being thrown out of college yet always managed to con his way back in. That's his game. He's a mouthpiece, a blagger, bullshitter extraordinaire. We sat there and recalled the time he insulted the head of the gay and lesbian society in the student bar. Connor had dared him to go up to her and suggest that if she put on a nice frock, grew her hair a bit, shaved her legs and chucked on some slap then she could quite feasibly get a seven out of ten for looks. Techno didn't need asking twice. And he told her. She played right into his hands, barking back, full throttle, while he shrugged wildly in mock-bewilderment, forcing back tears of laughter. She said she had no intention of looking attractive to a potential rapist like him, that she actually goes out of her way to look unavailable to the animal sex. To which he smiled, looked over at his boys, and told her she really didn't have to go to so much effort.

It was typical of the man, cruel, cocky, good value. He was Jack-the-lad, the fully-fledged cockney wide-boy, Londoner through and through. He had the broadest accent you've ever heard and an impressive line in self-confidence, which would certainly be an asset in Sales. He used to DJ at the student union once a week, under the pseudonym, *MC Planeterry*, his night subtly coined, '*A Licence to Pill*'. It was the most popular night of the week, until the plug was pulled after complaints it encouraged drug taking, and the students at our college needed very little encouragement on that score. It was a shame for Terry, he used to make a tidy sum from selling bags and pills from his booth during the longer remixes.

I was pleasantly surprised by his choice of career now. It certainly suited his brashness, with plenty of dosh to boot. Personally, I'd always thought he'd end up doing something a bit pathetic and dubious, off the back of a truck. I pictured him selling hot gear on street corners from an open suitcase: knock-off watches, fake designer clothing, watered down after-shave, one eye on PC Plod. But he'd exceeded expectations and was now smelling sweeter than most, and good on him for sharing a little of his newfound fortune with Connor. I had no real justification for my initial cynicism, apart from the fact he spent half his adult life hoovering all manner of chemicals up his beak and trying to scam his peers. But I'm not Connor's old man and therefore needed to stop sounding like a poorer version of him. They were mates, equals, who went way back. Like a lot of those types of friendships, they'd slipped apart, a natural mix of time and apathy. Until now, that is.

As we got up to leave I patted Connor on the shoulder and attempted to appease my guilt. 'It's great to have you back, Con.'

'It's great to *be* back, Sam,' he replied, 'and I'm okay, really I am. You can quit fretting, Pops. I know you mean well but I can look after myself now.'

We removed ourselves from the warmth of the café. Outside the sky was a mass of battleship grey.

The clouds looked fit to burst.

So we rushed home, trying our best to beat the oncoming storm.

14
Saturday night (five and a half months ago): 7:20pm

When Nicole was rushed to hospital I was left wondering if she was going to live or die. I was desperate. Those sorts of emotions don't surface all that often and until you suffer them you don't really know how you're going to react. Personally, I attempted to strike a deal with God. If he kept Nicole alive then, in return, we could lose the baby. Not nice I know but, as I said, I was desperate. I doubted if he'd be into bartering for the souls of unborn children. I just craved control. And I didn't want to lose Nicole. As it was, I lost her anyway.

When I got the news from the doctor, I wasn't surprised. And, yes, there was a part of me that was happy. I was happy that Nicole was alive. I was happy and devastated, both at the same time. I was desperate and confused. After all, I had lost my baby, too. I didn't have a miscarriage but I did lose my baby. Nicole had the miscarriage and I was left trying to be strong. That may sound hypocritical, after saying I'd gladly give up the baby to keep my girlfriend, but I am being honest. So how was Nicole feeling? I didn't know. She had just had her dead baby sucked out of her. It's hard to know what state that leaves you in.

From the moment Nicole suffered the miscarriage I felt like I was permanently on trial. I was slowly and deliberately running every word through my head, which made for a strained atmosphere. I was so concerned about saying something wrong, or saying something that could be twisted against me, I ended up saying very little at all. I was accused of not dealing with the real issues, of covering over the cracks. This, of course, was true. I was doing both those things. But I was doing them not because I was insensitive but because I wanted to avoid any more hurt for either of us. It was the wrong option but there was no manual to follow. In the end I was doing the one thing I was desperately trying to avoid, I was upsetting Nicole.

And as I blew more and more air into the cavity between us, so it grew beyond our control, turning into a monstrous wall of silence and apathy. Nicole thought I'd gone back to being emotionally stunted, that I'd reverted to kind, and therefore was no longer the person she'd fallen in love with. I feared that had I opened up then Nicole would have been so snowed under with negative emotion she'd have simply suffocated under the strain of it all, just like my mother. When she was at her lowest, her weakest and lightest, she still tried to be there for me, she wanted to make me talk. But she could bear no more, I could tell. It was all too weighty, too grave. So I left her. And I left Nicole, too.

I thought my job was to push the process along, lift Nicole up with a few positives, offer a window for the future, show how bright life could still be. At best I looked like a blithering fool with no grasp on reality; at worst I looked like an insensitive monster with no regard for his girlfriend. What had been my major concern on hearing the news of Nicole's pregnancy – namely the fact that my happiness would now be out of my control, that I was to be too reliant on the whims of fate – had suddenly come to be. My fear was now reality but I took no solace from the accuracy of my instinct.

When I saw her in hospital she looked different, and she looked at me differently. When the doctor finally let me in, Nicole shut me out. It was like walking into someone else's life. I wasn't pregnant. And until the world of science finally flips its lid, men never will be. Sure, we can boast that '*we're* pregnant', wear those empathy bumps, promise to be there every step of the way, to hold the hair back when they're sick, to fancy them when they're huge, to emulate their breathing and let them swear and blame us during labour. But men don't get pregnant.

It was her hormones adjusting to the onset of a new life. Essentially, I treated it all like a new hobby. I don't think fatherhood starts until the baby is born. You can prepare yourself, help create a personality for your child, but the true bonding begins when the two of you meet and interact for the first time. We know that boys do better at school when they learn in a hands-on fashion; we feel our way through things. When a baby's born, a knowing calm descends over its mother, she holds and looks for the first time but she's been feeling for ages. It's the new father who's screaming at the top of his lungs, buying drinks and doing cartwheels, shoving indistinct Polaroids into the faces of anyone who engages eye contact. That's his moment.

For me, that moment never came.

It was Nicole who felt the flutters, the kicks and the morning sickness. She was the one re-arranging her life to make way for our child. She had to give up alcohol and soft-boiled eggs, change her diet in accordance with a baby who was living, breathing and sleeping inside her. It was her life that was being turned upside-down, not mine, her career that was going to go on hold, her body that was preparing for unprecedented trauma and permanent change, expanding with a bump that moved and jolted her. Nicole already had a child whereas I was simply looking forward to seeing mine. I was desperate to see whom it looked like, to hold its tiny hand. I was looking forward whilst Nicole was living the dream. She felt like a mum. I felt like a kid.

And to have that promise physically wrenched away, to feel her baby relinquish its grasp on life whilst living under her charge; to have it unceremoniously ripped through her without so much as a scrap of dignity or hope; that damaged Nicole. As far as she was concerned she'd let her unborn child down. She was supposed to be in control and it was her responsibility to nurture that baby until it was strong enough to breath for itself in the outside world. And nothing I could say or do could help or change her mind. She didn't want me. She didn't want her mind changed. She wanted her baby. But her baby had died.

She had been carrying it everywhere she went for twenty weeks. She was so proud of that bump, grown to love it. She would push it out as far as it'd go and joke around, 'Look Sam, here's our baby, I'm *with child!*' Once, when I visited her in hospital after it all happened she asked me if I thought that her pushing out her bump had brought on the miscarriage. She was deadly serious. Through a wall of tears she begged me to tell her why it had happened. I told her it was nothing to do with that or anything else she had done. She finally stopped sobbing but I don't think she ever believed me, not really.

And then, within a matter of days, my old man tells me he's getting married. My mum never re-married. She didn't find it so easy to fall in love. Yet although the news of his impending marriage annoyed me for reasons that stretched back to my childhood, it wasn't the thing that *really* stirred my anger, that triggered my verbal assault. He also told me he was planning on starting a family. Start a fucking family? How about finishing one first, how about getting ours right before screwing up another one? Or was that the idea? We were the rough draft, the practice run, the fucking dress rehearsal.

My own scars were still tender. I'd just had my one and only chance seized from me. Granted, I'd not exactly enthused early on but I was getting ready, ridding myself of the insecurities he'd help instill. Now *he* wanted another go. Not only did he want another chance at being a proper father, he wanted my blessing. What he got was my wrath. I threw everything I had at him.

My first reaction to something that is potentially exciting or good is to worry. Big time. After the initial concern I'm usually fine, once it's out of my system. I've been like this since I was a child. And it was following my parents' break-up that I started to suspect the really good things don't last forever. It's not unreasonable for a teenage kid to expect his family unit to remain intact while he grows up inside it. So when mine capitulated around me I was understandably peeved. It took the wind out of my sails at a time when those sails were just about coping with the stormy waters of the onset of manhood. I was a boy. The one person I thought I should try and grow into, my dad, had just dismantled my slender grasp on the world. Suddenly I had no one to live up to, no one to be like. My dad was my role model, my provider, my rock; suddenly I had to rebuild my value system, rebuild my life, this time with walls, and barbed wire, and no light.

It's not easy, rebuilding in a battlefield. It wasn't a noisy, ammo-filled, exploding battlefield. It was more like one of those war movies, post-battle, where all that's left is a crumbling, smoking, corpse of a city, de-stabilised buildings, no sign of life save for the odd sniper hiding in the shadows, waiting for a clear shot at someone's back. Our home fell silent, murky and dusty. Everyone began to withdraw, offering only nods and glances, each one trying to survive, searching for space and shelter. My mother was visibly wilting. She did her best to shade us from flying shrapnel but it was a bit like trying to fend off a meteor shower with an umbrella.

The anxiety that built slowly was a signpost to the crescendo of rage that inevitably followed, so predictable; so torturous in its inevitability, that it only succeeded in draining yet more life from our home. I remember buying albums with a view to blocking out the next row. The heavier the atmosphere, the heavier the music. Anything was better than all that sniping.

I started to feel separate emotions for each parent. Previously I had treated them as a unit. Suddenly I was feeling pity for my mother and anger towards my father. Like the proverbial alley cat he had strayed away from home and, despite her best efforts, my mum could not find it in her heart to forgive him and carry on. I no longer had the option of being under the same roof as both my parents, so I stayed with mum and watched her cave. I saw my dad at weekends and talked to him without saying anything of great significance. We went to the football or the rugby or to a gig or a show. We needed the background noise and the visual distraction to save the awkwardness of it all. I never asked for an explanation or an apology despite still feeling like one or both would somehow have made my life easier. After a lifetime of marriage my father had traded everything we had for a lewd fumble on the casting couch with some scrubber half his age. He broke up the family without employing a single shred of originality. The village was full of men like him, and women like my poor mother.

The commuters on that train from Hamesly-on-Thames to Waterloo Station always looked so dispassionate and uninteresting, like they'd been ceremoniously drained of their individuality. Yet there was one middle-aged man on that train who stood out. He never wore a suit, he smoked tabs on the platform, read the tabloids, wore plenty of gold and labels and shone like a star against the gloomy backdrop of pin stripes and paisley.

My dad.

And I was proud of him. Well, I was, until the day he took that pride and rammed it down our communal throats. He part-owned a model agency in Covent Garden, following fashion but never the crowd. He craved the new and the fresh, never dwelling on the old or the tired. I hate being restricted, he'd say. I thought

119

that was great, so cool. When I was growing up I was happy to sit with my dad on the train. Some kids would rather die. Not me. I was dead proud. My dad acted young. He didn't want to grow old, grow up or grow out. He went to New Order gigs, stood on the terraces at Chelsea, wore Ralph Lauren and kept his notes in a solid gold money clip. Middle age would never paralyse him, I thought.

And I was right.

It didn't.

He slept with one of the models from work and handed his son a divorce for his fourteenth birthday. He traded the family home for the casting couch and suddenly looked more sad old bastard than trendy role model. He'd tried to be a mate, when what I needed was a dad. I had mates, like Connor. It was a different job altogether. The life soon drained from our bond. We were no good at being serious with each other. I'd always behaved myself so as not to upset him, it was our deal, reliant on his style and my maturity. There'd never been the need for more structure or hierarchy than that. Suddenly I was desperate for parental control and guidance, but my options were limited, and my development was arrested.

My reaction to the news of Nicole's pregnancy was trained by my past, tainted by personal history. This is not an excuse, a reason, or an answer; it's just true. When all the tension had conjoined, Nicole and I rowed, made up, then split up. A few months down the track, Connor saw her in town, arm in arm with the new guy. Toby. Primary School teacher, like Nicole, just what she'd always wanted, someone so in touch with his feminine side he'd forgotten which gender he belonged to. He was obviously an all-rounder, able to juggle a paintbrush, a game of rounders and a Good News bible all in the same afternoon. I bet he avoided his comfort zone like the plague. I didn't know how serious they were; all I knew is they'd been 'close friends' for a while now, whatever that meant. She used to mention him but I didn't think much of it at the time. I wondered what else she'd said that I didn't really hear.

Connor had spotted them together twice. On the second occasion they were falling out of The Red Lion, giggling and cuddling, probably laughing at the fact that her 'ex' never enjoyed public shows of affection, that he always insisted on drinking in The Fox and Hounds, with its dodgy locals and time-warped decor. I was clinging to the faint hope that he was a serial bore or a closet homosexual, a married philanderer or a eunuch (definitely a eunuch) or anything else that would eventuate in the rapid breakdown of their relationship. I didn't want Nicole hurt, just slightly miffed. Slightly miffed at not being able to find a suitable replacement for me. I once thought it might be good if Nicole went out with some sad git who compared badly to me. Now I wasn't so sure.

The worst thing was that I knew, I just knew, he was the type of sad git who was in total control of his emotions. He could control them like a yo-yo champion. While I, on the other hand, was controlling mine with all the poise and dexterity of a one-armed wallpaper hanger.

15
Monday: 1:23pm

We got back inside the house only seconds before a deep roll of thunder reverberated all around us. Moments later the heavens unleashed a torrential downpour that hit the ground so hard it bounced off the pavement and back into the swirling wind. The rain pounded impressively against the kitchen window as I watched the street below surrender to the irresistible will of nature. Car headlights came on, beams illuminating the ferocity of the falling rain; vehicles slowing as pools of water wrapped themselves around tyres, and pedestrians ran for cover, grasping umbrellas that surged and folded under the strain of a playful wind.

I put the kettle on and took three cups off the mug tree. Surprisingly, each of our favourite mugs was clean and dry. We'd given the flat a thorough tidy in anticipation of Connor's return and I felt good about making a brew for the three of us again. It was symbolic of a fresh start for all of us. My special mug had Chelsea Football Club emblazoned on it; Connor's had a picture of George from *Seinfeld* and Donnie had one with a photo of Perth taken from King's Park at night.

His mum had bought it as a leaving present all those years ago, correctly presuming he'd have more hot drinks over here. She'd given it the night before he left; with tears of pride and imminent loss welling in her eyes she said, 'You might be going over there to find your roots, but don't forget the place where you grew and blossomed.' London had always been a magnet to Donnie. His mother was worried the two might stick a little too tight. She was right to worry, but wrong to think he'd stay forever.

We sat in the front room with an open packet of chocolate digestives and raised a toast to Connor, welcoming him back home and wishing him luck with his job interview. Our mugs clinked and we settled down for a chat in front of MTV. When it was time for Connor to get ready we helped him on with his suit, struggled not to laugh at his chicken legs and sent him on his way. Donnie hung around for a while but eventually admitted he too had arranged to be elsewhere. Unsurprisingly he was due to meet Amber the model. He spruced himself up, cooked up a round of bacon butties and sloped out. As he opened the door to leave I asked him if he'd be home later. He said he wasn't sure (which obviously meant no). Then I asked him if she was his girlfriend and he said he wasn't sure of that either (which obviously meant yes). He simply winked, and I agreed to see him after work tomorrow.

It was just me, the History Channel, and a heady stench of freshly dabbed aftershave. I was just about to choose between an afternoon sleep and a hot bath with loud music when the phone rang. I sat upright in my chair and turned the volume on the TV right down. I tend to screen most calls these days, even if I've got an idea who it's going to be, but four thirty on a Monday afternoon is prime screening time. As the message - Connor doing an impression of Sean Connery – ended and the beeps kicked in, I convinced myself it would be someone from school ready to hassle me on my day off about a missing lesson plan or an enraged parent. So, naturally, I panicked. But it wasn't work; it was Nicole. So I panicked even more.

As she began to leave her message I leapt awkwardly for the handset, stumbling headfirst into the coffee table. The remote control went flying across the living room and the footstool I'd been using knocked over the tray of mugs onto the newly vacuumed carpet. The room was a sea of biscuit crumb confetti and tea-dreg puddles. Yet still I scrambled. I grabbed the phone at arm's length and the line immediately snaked itself around my neck, but asphyxiation by telephone cord was not going to stand between me and a conversation with Nicole.

I got there just in time to take a deep breath and put on my best phone-voice. Determined not to let the chaos of the last ten seconds resonate my manner, I exhaled, empowering myself in the process. I'd be the essence of calm, composure and masculinity. As Ollie Hardy used to say, she'd be *none the wiser*.

'Hey Nicole, how's it going?'

'Hi Sam. Are you okay, you sound a bit flustered?'

Hmm.

'Sam? You still there?'

'Yeah, sorry.'

'How are you?'

'Yeah, you know, just chilling.'

Seeing as Nicole read me like a soppy novel anyway, I guessed I may as well be straight. And I figured the best way of doing this was to talk to her like I used to when we were together, try and relocate our level, ignite the old spark. So I answered her question as if I was one half of the impenetrable twosome of old.

'How am I? I'm all the better for hearing your silky tone.'

It was a risky little game. But I was determined to stop the conversation deteriorating into one of those standard post-break-up chats, watered down and overly courteous, sprinkled with subtle dishonesties and little white lies. This is how I would've been before, half serious, unfettered, comfortable. There was a definite pause. I knew it, it was all too brazen, too obvious and throwaway, typical of a man who thinks responsibility begins and ends with getting his round in.

'You obviously took your charm pill this morning, then.'

Still alive.

'I've started a new dose, actually. Well, same as I used to take.'

'Oh yeah, why you on those again?'

'Seems like a good time.'

'I thought Connor was the cryptic one.'

'To be honest, I just wanted to try being normal again.'

'What do you mean, *again*?'

'You know what I mean.'

'I guess so. Like the old days, huh?'

'Something like that.'

'Cool.'

'So when are we going to meet up again? I'd really like to see you.'

'Hang on there, Mr Assertive. Give a girl a chance.'

'Sorry, it's just that yesterday was nice. I'd like to do it again, that's all.'

'Well, I guess that would be okay. I had a good time too.'

'So how about a drink then, just the two of us? We've got a lot to talk about.'

'Do we?'

'Of course we do. How about going down The Fox on Friday night, for old time's sake?'

'That sounds awfully like a date to me.'

'Do you want it to be?'

'No.'

'Has that bothered you?'

'I don't know. I'm feeling a bit weird about all this to be honest with you, Sam.'

'Okay. No date, no strings, just a couple of old friends catching up. What do you say?'

'But that's the thing, Sam. We're not just old friends, are we?'

'No, I'd like to think we were a lot more than that, which is precisely why we should be able to meet up without it turning into anything weird. Come on, just me and you, a couple of drinks and a bit of a laugh.'

'Fair enough. But Sam … '

'Yes?'

'Can we go somewhere else? I wouldn't mind a bit of neutral territory.'

'You make it sound like a battleground.'

'That's what I'm trying to avoid.'

'It used to be your local too, you know.'

'No, Sam, it was always *our* local.'

We arranged to meet at eight o' clock on Friday night at Scooters, one of the new breed of bar, with mock-wood flooring, leather sofas, morning papers, coffee machine, complimentary nuts on the bar, and good-looking bar staff who wear neatly pressed green aprons and give your change back in a wooden bowl. Whether all that's worth an extra fifty per cent on the price of a bottle of lager is arguable but I thought it was a good choice for a meeting, or a date. That's the beauty of a pub date: you can always find one to match your mood. If you're after carpet that's as thick as the bar staff and a jukebox that still plays the best of *Wham* then look no further than The Fox and Hounds. The only nuts you're likely to get on the bar there is during one of Sandra's infamous ladies' nights. Last year's event was reduced to mayhem when a flock of sexed up, overripe female onlookers made a beeline for the male stripper's lunchbox. The poor bastard was forced to scramble over the bar, completely starkers save for a bow tie and sleeveless cuffs, his buffed torso gleaming with the sting of baby oil and talon scrapes. Those nuts were only on the bar for the briefest of moments and were far from being complimentary.

I knew more than ever I wanted to cajole Nicole back into my half-baked existence. And this date, meeting, whatever, was as good a place to start as any. I also knew that it would be far from easy but I had the advantage of history on my side, not to mention my secret weapon: a female friend. And although I was sure Toby the teacher had female friends flying out of his arsehole, I was fairly certain he wasn't on first name terms with anyone quite as conniving as Abby North.

Our fateful reunion had proved the juncture I needed. I already had the game plan and the necessary skill levels in order to impress Nicole, I'd proven that before. What I needed now was a fresh set of tactics, a new perspective, some inside information on the opposition.

So, after daydreaming about Nicole, I called Abby North.

She was off on Tuesday night so we arranged to meet. Trouble was, I was running out of pubs. The Fox and Hounds was sacred ground. The Red Lion had been irrevocably tarnished after Toby the teacher was spotted dragging Nicole out of there. That just left Scooters within acceptable walking distance. Ideally I didn't want to jinx myself by going there before Friday but caved in due to the lack of a satisfactory alternative.

I was banking on Abby. I explained to her my need for some life-altering advice and she said she'd sort me out for the cost of a couple of large glasses of Chardonnay. Bargain, I thought. Toby the teacher was reciting his last metaphysical poem.

The only problem now was what to wear?

16
Monday: 6:19pm

The next thing I remember was Connor tapping me on the shoulder, upsetting my afternoon slumber. It wasn't the first time I'd fallen asleep in front of the TV of late. It seemed not even the thrill of a date with Nicole could halt my march toward middle age. There was even a telltale trace of dribble on my chin and a few crisp crumbs balancing precariously on the crest of my stomach.

Connor was wearing a savage grin and holding two cans of lager.

'I got it, Sam.'

'The job?'

'Yep.'

'Fantastic news, mate.'

'Thanks.'

'So what happened?'

I sat up, wiped the drool from my chin, brushed the grit off my shirt and looked at the can of lager. I'd just stirred from a cavernous sleep, had a mouth like a rabbit hutch, a lump of hurt where my nose used to be and it was barely teatime on a school night. Beer? Why not? Surprisingly, the thought of slugging back on a cold one was far from unpleasant. I grabbed it off him, cracked the little devil open and sunk a couple of hefty draughts. It sailed down without fuss. The taste of success was sweet and hoppy, life was looking up for both of us.

We drank to new horizons and Connor walked me through his afternoon.

'I think Techno Terry put in a few good words for me. I thought he might have been exaggerating about how important he was to the firm but he seems to be quite well known there. I just talked a bit about myself, mentioned a few things about the company that Techno had told me, threw in a few big words and half an hour later they're offering me a trial period.'

'Congratulations mate, talk about turning your life around.'

'You snooze, you lose, that's my motto.'

'Since when?'

'It's new.'

'So what do you do then?'

'Basically, I sell drugs.'

'What?'

'You know, medication, to doctors and that. We deal in tablets for high blood pressure mostly, essential hypotension, that sort of thing. I pitch to GPs and try and get them to buy from us. Eventually we get a car, laptop, mobile phone, all paid for. It's a top job Sam and it's got prospects galore. But it's long hours, especially while they're training me up.'

'Sounds just the ticket. When do you start?'

'Training starts the day after tomorrow.'

'Where's it based?'

'They've got these flash offices on Hampton Road, not far from here. Techno Terry's picking me up on Wednesday morning at eight o' clock.'

With that Connor thrust three sluggish-looking textbooks into my lap. I yelped a little under the weight but tried to look suitably spellbound. They had no pictures, only diagrams of hearts and veins and other bits and pieces I couldn't make out. They talked of blood pressure and the products you need if it's too high or too low or too buggered by booze and cigarettes. When my interest had waned irreversibly I offered to fetch another couple of tinnies. Connor was genuinely excited and I was excited for him. I was also glad I taught English and not Science.

He had been wasting away at that video shop; he had so much to offer but whenever he tried to push any new ideas or innovations his boss just told him to concentrate on smiling to the customer and making the queues smaller. He was using his degree and, more to the point, appeared visibly upbeat about the whole thing. And that in itself was a miracle after the weekend we'd just had.

I told him about my conversation with Nicole and he cheered out loud. Then he went to the fridge and got out two more beers, which we sank with ease, safe in the knowledge our luck, like student milk, was on the turn. We had a couple more and then turned in. We knew Donnie would be spending the night with Amber the model and this meant (if he was any kind of a man) he too would be enjoying a positive experience. It had been a fair while since all three of us had ended a day on such a high note.

17
Tuesday: 7:36am

The next morning soon barged its way into my subconscious, triggering mild irritation and reluctant acknowledgment of the job at hand. As per usual, it took a while for my brain to convince my body that it couldn't get to work on its own, that it had to be a collaborative effort. Once up, my morning routine is both well established and mildly efficient, though propped up by a reliance on caffeine, nicotine and boiling water. I try to do everything in twenty minutes. Then I walk for five, grind onto the tube for seven, before marching the final four to school.

Normally I ignore the ugly horde of Year 10 skaters chucking jumps off their makeshift half pipe round the corner from Churchfields High. I refuse to tell anyone off unless I have to, more out of apathy than some trendy notion of ownership or liberty. But today I'm feeling mildly sociable, which takes me by surprise, and am drawn to the delightful waft of cigarette smoke emanating from the bus shelter which doubles up as a viewing gallery for hormonal female onlookers. I walk over and bum a tab off a girl called Miranda who I know as a smart student who cares little for the subtle nuances of English literature. She once got quite excited about Sylvia Plath but that worried me even more. As she smiles the braces on her teeth glint in the morning sunshine. It's cold, but good weather. We talk about TV and about other teachers, slagging off both in equal measure. She smokes Marlboro Lights, a trendy cigarette, lacking that chest-gravel quality I usually crave. She's obviously addicted to the look and idea of smoking, which is fair enough. I'm sure her Friday night heels are equally damaging, crippling her freshly-painted toes, but still eminently worth wearing. They call me Smithy, which I like. When we get back to school they'll revert back to Mr Smith, which I appreciate too, without acknowledging.

They're good kids, really.

Churchfields High is a sanctuary for comfort zoners like myself. It's situated in a fairly high socio-economic area; the majority of fathers are still at home, there's a good attendance record and an encouragingly compliant parent body; all making for a well-adjusted, low maintenance student faction, all without the unnecessary burden of a private school curriculum.

There's the odd head-case, screw-up or time waster but I've learned to spot them early. They get fast-tracked to the relevant authority pretty sharpish; a quick buck-pass to Admin, a brief mock-panicky phone call to social services, a firm shove in the direction of the trendy student counsellor or a persuasive word in the ear of the green-gilled graduate with more ambition than sense; each one sufficiently dispatched before becoming too familiar with my apron strings. Otherwise, if you let them in, you have to be responsible for them. And the paperwork's a pain. There's the IEP, the BMS, the extra

PD. So many acronyms, so little time. A lot of BS, really. Parent contacts, follow-up calls. Unrewarded effort. Very overrated. Goodwill's a thankless burden I'm not prepared to shoulder these days. Not with the mood I'm in.

I get in at 8:25am, exactly five minutes before I legally have to. Add that up over a whole school year and I think you'll find I'm one of life's doers, putting in the hard yards on a daily basis. I get in early. Every day. Fact. Then I drink tea, eat pastry and surf the net. But still I get there early.

The morning is bright, impatient in its glare. The beads of sweat that form on my forehead are an irritating product of my break in routine; the chat and ciggie were nice, but made for a smarter than usual hike into school. This coupled by the unseasonable warmth make for a scratchy mood. Still, Tuesdays are relatively good for me this year as I start with a free. I bluff and wing my way through Monday, loosely programming the rest of the week first thing Tuesday morning.

The English office is a blur of activity, annoying me still further. The copier is strumming away in the corner and there's all manner of temple rubbing and chest beating going on. Fat women gossip and slurp, their plumage ruffling at the thought of another day of power tripping, their lives beginning and ending with the school bell. Chubby calves poke out of pleated tartan skirts, swishing uncomfortably as I pass. I throw out a few half-hearted nods and make a beeline for my desk, hoping Paddy is already there, feeling as lackadaisical as me. He's asleep at his desk, which immediately perks me up. Paddy is the only other English teacher I get on with. Mags, our Head of Department, is great, a peripheral friend, but knows very little about football or television and refuses to discuss the sexual habits of fellow staffers. Paddy specializes in Media and spends far too much of his life up late, watching crap and smoking dope. The kids love him, and he's good, too. When he's awake. I ruffle his powdery brown hair, immediately noticing the speed at which it is retreating back down his scalp. Again, I feel better. My hair is thick, black and holding up well. I crop it pretty short, apply a modicum of wax and work hard at making it look naturally unkempt. I do get the odd telltale spike of grey stubble when I leave it too long between shaves but generally I'm happy with the whole hair and face set up. And judging by the state of Paddy's mug, it could be worse. He's only a couple of years older but looks more, and would no doubt benefit from a month of sleep and a Swedish nanny. He's already got a couple of sprogs and his missus is pregnant with a third. High School often acts as a contraceptive for teachers but Paddy seems determined to fill his house with little versions of himself. He recounts daily horror stories of sleepless nights and nuclear nappies; his desk is awash with photos and drawings and he drinks industrial strength coffee from a mug with 'World's Greatest Dad' proudly adorned on it. He never complains though, not really. And, when conscious, he's happy, happy with his lot.

'Sammy. Shit, must have nodded off there, fella.'

'How are you?'

'Bit buggered, old son. Bit like your snout. What happened?'

'Long story.'

When the bell rings the whole room erupts in a wave of corduroy and coffee breath. Some waddle, some whinge, some laugh gleefully at the prospect of reasserting themselves at the expense of the odd twelve-year-old child, and they all pile out the office in search of fresh meat and old lessons. The room falls beautifully quiet, doubling in size, quadrupling in stillness. Soon it's just the smell of old textbooks and me. I've got forty-five minutes to sort myself out. I make a brew and boot up my laptop. The planning can wait; I've got websites to visit, starting with e-mail. Stunned excitement washes over me as I'm told of eight new messages in my inbox. Then, as if to mock my recurrent impercipience, it's revealed that none of them are from people who know me. Penis enlargement leads the way, closely followed by debt consolidation, hair renewal and impotency cures. It's hard not to get paranoid during moments like this. Then, after a quick stop and search through my favoured sites, I prepare my week's lessons. It takes me a record nine minutes; an eclectic mix of novel study, journalism, print advertising and Haiku. Those lucky little bastards. Efficient time management is the backbone of successful programming. For the rest of the time I decompress and look forward to Friday night. My mental preparation starts here – garment choice, hair tactics, maximum use of the Abby factor, it all needs sorting upstairs first. Only then can I work on discourse and anecdotal reference. I also phone Connor to see how he is. Chirpy as ever, watching *The Sopranos* on DVD. Then, as if to complete the circle, I call Donnie who, after a tumultuous night on the nest, is running late for work. Fair enough. When you sleep with a model, who gets up early?

I have two visitors during my free period, both students. One is a very pretty Year 12 girl, named

Camomile, who passes me a note sent from Mr Callard, our Head of PE and chief letch. I know, almost immediately, that the note is bogus. Callard has done this before, using a false message as a pretext to show off a particularly well-endowed eighteen-year-old female student. Once a term he'll spot some busty young filly before sending her off on a wild goose chase round campus. Her job is to show said note to a select faction of male staff, whilst unwittingly showing them her wares. The note reads: *'Messyrs Morris, Smith, Thomas and Wilkinson, don't forget the important meeting today, there's at least TWO things we need to discuss. Regards, John Callard, PE Dept and Chairman of CGDC.'*

The CGDC is the Churchfields Gentlemen's Drinking Club of which I am a proud member. Donnie and Connor are honorary affiliates, passing the initiation ceremony without difficulty (it involved a little nakedness and lot of drinking – proving a breeze for both.)

This isn't a test of my professionalism. I've told Callard before that I find such games distasteful. Now he does it to annoy me. But I don't care enough to get annoyed. I should probably down tools and march to the PE shed, demanding my name be scrubbed from the list of seedy subscribers to a club that is juvenile and unprincipled. I am not annoyed, just uninterested. I taught this girl when she was younger and - it has to be said - much smaller. But she's still a kid, even if she doesn't feel like one, even though she's trying her best to stretch and strain and fly into adulthood, before she's fully grown. And despite all the eye make-up, the winks and the flutters, she's flying blind. Young Camomile has no chance of prizing my interest. Not in that way at least. And my indifference appears to annoy. As she turns to leave, she releases a short, huffy sigh, followed by a monumental eye roll, and then disappears down the corridor in search of a more accommodating member of staff.

The second visit is much more serious. It arrives in the form of a weary looking boy with greasy hair and bubbling eyes. He storms into the office, demanding my interest. I look up. He's wearing a beat-up denim jacket and baseball cap, good labels, nicely worn. But before I get the chance to commend him on his choice of garments, he shouts at me. 'Oi, mister, who do I have to call an arsehole round here to get suspended?'

You get a lot of bizarre questions in this job, on a daily basis. This one was up there with the best. Still, it deserved an honest answer.

'You'll need to go a bit higher than me, pal. Headmaster's office is down the hall.'

'Cheers.'

And with that he went.

I was at a bit of a loss. I've been in the teaching game for a good number of years now but have never been asked anything like that. It made sense; if you really want out, then call someone important an *arsehole*. My initial reaction was to stay out of it, not to get involved. It had paperwork written all over it. More paperwork than the morning after a hot curry. But something made me move. It wasn't annoyance, nor was it a desire for personal justice. It was more complex than that. I felt something I hadn't felt in the job for ages: compassion, gut feeling. I think it was the way he said 'cheers', the residue of politeness hovering above the gruff, troubled manner. There was definitely something there, in him or in me. Something I used to spot or have, before I discarded my radar in favour of ignorance.

I made a few calls – student counsellor, student records. They gave me the relevant password and I logged into the school system. His name was Rory Holland. It was his second day at school and everyone knew him already. And then I saw something very interesting. To everyone else having a gander at his record it would have meant little. To me, it meant everything. Empathy, sympathy, bewilderment. It's funny what a few words can do, especially when you're not ready to read them.

His address was in Hamesley-on-Thames, my old village.

His stepfather, Rodney Smith.

My dad.

Immediately, I jumped from my seat and went looking for the rude little wanker.

Tuesday, 9:47am

He wasn't hard to track down.

Like so many in his position, he wanted to be found, and he wanted to be heard. He was sitting, smoking, inside the PE shed. Callard was busting balls on the rugby field and Rory had the place to himself. I came straight out with it.

'Your stepfather?'

'What about him?'

'Does he own a model agency?'

'Yeah, lucky arsehole.'

That word again. It was unnerving me, the ease with which he threw it around in the company of a teacher, an elder, a stranger.

'He's my old man.'

'Bollocks.'

'It's true.'

'He's nothing to me. He'll never be my dad.'

'Don't you like him?'

'I do. He's okay. Why, don't you?'

'You're right. He's okay.'

'Cigarette?'

'Why not.'

I wasn't sure whether I was working him over, working him out or leaning on him for information. Whatever. We talked and I liked him. And he liked my dad, a lot. He just hated the fact his real one had died last week in a car smash. It turned out that, until recently, he'd been at boarding school, choosing to live away from home following the break-up of his parents. But after his mother got together with my flirtatious father, ten months ago, he began to like home again. He'd arranged to start at Churchfields a couple of weeks ago, before his dad had the accident. My dad had suggested it, said it had an excellent reputation, great teachers. Silver-tongued rogue.

Rory was hurting. But he just didn't know what to do with the pain. I had a plan. It felt good to be feeling the job again. The only problem: it meant speaking to my old man. However, my issues on that score suddenly felt lukewarm and small. First I needed to start the protocol rolling. His mum, who until now had just been my father's latest shag piece, one whom I'd never met but had been informed as to her desire to father him a prototype child, hadn't informed the school of the incident, at Rory's request. Which, no offence or anything, was a pretty stupid decision.

I sat him at my desk, gave him a coffee and a Danish, contacted his form tutor and Head of Year, and phoned his mother, who promised to collect him at once. Then, I grabbed my mobile, sought the solitude of our interview room and called his stepfather. It rang maybe half a ring.

'Sam?' It was a good tone, like he was holding down excitement with a cushion.

'Dad, how's things?'

'Pretty good, yeah, mustn't grumble, son, how about yourself?'

'Yeah, okay. Listen, this isn't really a social one, I'm at school. With Rory.'

'Right, right. Probably should have called about that though, eh.'

'Probably.'

'Didn't think you'd run into the boy quite yet. Is he okay?'

He was nervous and, yes, part of me was enjoying the squirming of a guy whose cool was legendary, but highly overrated.

'Well, I have run into him and he told me about his dad. He's pretty messed up and I think we need to deal.'

'Course, Sam. It's been a heavy time, you know. Didn't know which way to play it, to be frank. At a bit of a loss to tell the truth, son. Rory's a top guy, breaks your heart, really does.'

'He *is* a good guy. Thinks the world of you.'

'Ah, really? Yes, the boy's like a, you know, we're cool, Rory and I.'

'His mum was good, too, very supportive.'

'Diane? Yes, you'd really, um, she's great, hit her hard too, mind. Listen, Sam, any chance of a quiet beer sometime, bit to talk about.'

'Yes. We need to talk about the right course of action for Rory. I've taken him on, informed his form tutor and HoD. I've got some strategies, avenues I'd like to try.'

'Tonight?'

'Yeah okay, oh, no, can't, sorry, not tonight.'

'Seeing a girl, eh?'

'Kind of.'

'*Kind of.* Transvestite is he?'

'Funny. No, it's a proper girl, just not a date.'

'Wow, since when did you have friends who are girls?'

'I haven't. Yet.'

'Hey?'

'Long story, Dad.'

'How's Nicole?'

'That one's even longer.'

We promised to meet soon. To talk about Rory. When I returned to my desk, he was still there, which was a good sign. I had his trust. I had given him the opportunity to flee, but instead he had chosen to stick it out, and had, inadvertently, begun to own his problems, which was the first step towards solving them. Then a call came through for me. Rory's mother had arrived to take him home.

It was time to meet my father's old slag of a girlfriend.

18
Tuesday: 9:32 am

Nice lady. Warmish, classy, well aware of whom I was, what I meant. To be fair, Diane was highly personable. We talked only briefly: about Rory's morning, his need for a few quiet days, a couple of basic strategies - interpersonal stuff, active listening – as well as my embryonic plan.

She was good looking, past her sell-by date by a year or two, no more, late thirties I'd say. Dressed her age, which is so important. She'd clearly been crying, more teary-eyed than suicidal, which was understandable given the state of play. I felt sorry for my mum, again, but knew she was okay these days, with her book club, her evening soapies, her games of Bridge and her wine and cheese do's. She even had a gentleman friend – Norman, whom she courted in commendably old school fashion. But she wasn't planning on extending her family. She'd done a handsome job with the first lot, if you ask me.

When the final bell rang for the end of the school day I turned my attention to tonight's meeting with Abby. I went home, ate a microwave meal-for-one, watched the news, showered, drained two cans of Heineken and felt

143

glad I wasn't relying on either of my flatmates for company this evening. Connor was out talking textbooks with Techno Terry, while Donnie was working late, wheeling and dealing with the money of people who didn't really need any more but would take it if it's going.

Despite having over three hours to get there I arrive at Scooters a little late. When I enter I find Abby intermingling and giggling with the smarmy Mediterranean barman whom I'd clocked before. I had him sussed. To my mind - and I have an excellent record when it comes to instantaneous, unfounded pigeon-holing - he has no proper male friends, instead choosing to prowl alone in search of vulnerable, hardboiled old hags, or in this case, breasty young nurses. His southern European accent is dubious, his desire to infect Abby's personal space insatiable. I know it's not a date, but still.

'Sorry I'm a bit late.'

'That's okay, Marco's been keeping me busy, I mean, company.'

'Has he now?'

Marco is wearing a tight white shirt that has buttons he chooses not to use. He glistens in all the right places and, as if to compound suspicion, chooses to ignore me for as long as he can get away with.

'Bottle of Bud, please mate.'

Still he flirts.

'When you're ready, barman.'

Judging by the rampant groundcover of his five o'clock shadow, I feel sure Marco owns a fairly hairy back, which makes me feel better.

Still he disregards me.

I'm both parched and wound up, a potentially perilous cocktail.

'Look, pal, I'm still waiting over here? Or is it pour-your-own night tonight?

'Staredy orn, my flend, wot eeze dis? I was jus' tokkin' to *your* geelflend. You 'ave zer pleasure of 'er all evan-ing. Me, I get but a flayting mo-ment.'

Abby loves this.

Despite having the vocal equivalent of a fake tan, Marco's gusset dampening drawl leaves her tongue lounging. He slams down a tepid bottle of lager on the mock mahogany bar top without transferring his gaze, flattening his outstretched palm in readiness of my hard earned. The bottle ejaculates, dribbling pathetically as I grip its neck. I pay and promptly retreat. Abby reluctantly agrees to join me in the corner. As I turn Marco mumbles something about a 'gleen-eyed monstare' but, like all good chalkies, I choose to ignore the poor behaviour.

Abby is the type of girl who, with the insistent passing of time, will inevitably be described as a 'handsome woman.' It's all there, the shapely bumps, the dirty smile, the pedestrian metabolic rate. She asks me if she's changed much in the time between meetings. Obviously, I lie. No, not in the slightest. Don't get me wrong, she's still very shaggable, but we all change. I know I have. Her personality is still as invigorating as ever, mind you, but she didn't mean that.

She makes me laugh, reminding me of moments I'd lost; moments I'd substituted, surpassed, wrongly so. We drink and talk, each round softening us still further, granting more candid reminiscing, less cringing. Marco is a tool, I conclude. Each time I venture to the bar he appears less hospitable. And, once suitably oiled, I tell him so. First I suggest he work his way up to bottle washer before looking down his nose at customers. Then, on my next shout, I ask if he needs help fastening his shirt buttons. He finally cracks; describing me, in what I presume is his real accent - the brand of estuary English usually reserved for villains on *The Bill* and Techno Terry - as a 'cocky big-nosed wanker.' I presume he is referring to my recently broken snout. So I lean in across the bar and into his face and whisper, Sharkhead style.

'You're not called Marco at all, are you?'

'What?'

'It's Mark, isn't it?'

'Careful, mate, or I'll have you barred.'

'What for, calling you by your proper name?'

It's good fun, and I look forward to reporting back to Donnie and Connor later. I leave Mark, thwarted and broken, and return to my friend. As far as gleaning priceless tactical information in lieu of Friday night, she proves helpful, if not spectacular. She bleated on about honesty and integrity but gave little by way of killer lines or trade secrets. Still, I felt glad to have a friend on the inside. And it'd been fun, more than a business meeting, without the emotional implication.

The only moment of awkwardness occurred during the closing stages of the evening. It may have been those feelings of familiarity, the reminiscing, the renaissance of routine or the simple work of booze. Whatever the trigger, Abby lunged at me, mouth agape, in search of a spot of tonsil tennis, possibly followed by some bedroom athletics and the inevitable break-up of our friendship. I saw it coming and turned it into a hug.

Nothing was said. We'd survived our first outing as mates, reasonably intact. In a way, it was nice to know I could still draw a half-desperate pounce from a half-cut handsome woman. It was something else to tell the boys.

As we leave I throw a hollow farewell at Mark the barman, within full earshot of Abby. He quickly reverts to character.

'Wot iz dis *Mark* biziness, eh?'

Abby begins to froth.

'See you Marco,' she purrs. 'Ooh, I love those Latin types, me.'

For the next couple of days life rolls by without notable incident. I spend my time thinking about my date with Nicole, contemplating whether I can get away with calling her before Friday night. I don't want to look overly keen, setting off alarm bells, losing ground. On the other hand I want to maintain momentum and make it look as much like a real date as possible without actually using the word. In the end I figure I can phone on Thursday afternoon and disguise it as a confirmation call.

Breakfast time was becoming a bizarre event in our household. For the past couple of mornings we'd congregated around the table at around 7:30am, Connor in his new suit, Donnie in one of his older, flashier ones, and me in whatever I'd chosen to wear that wasn't in with a chance of getting an airing on Friday night. Connor had always worked shifts so we hadn't had much in the way of communal breakfasts before. Previously to that we'd been students and breakfast time had been a myth that real people talked about. Suddenly we *were* those people. The three of us sat there, eating cereal and discussing the prospects of the day. Then, to add to the general abnormality, Techno Terry would pull up in his flash motor and his finest clobber to pick Connor up. We'd then go our separate ways, promising to catch up later. Obviously we would keep in touch via mobiles and office phones throughout the working day, but it was nice to set a date for teatime. It gave a bit of extra structure to our day.

Thursday: 1pm

I decided to call Nicole during her lunch-break, hoping she wasn't on playground duty. I felt sad I no longer knew when her duties were. I used to be privy to all that sort of information, staff meetings, parents' nights, conferences, sports days, excursions. I wondered whether Toby knew as much as I did. Then remembered he was a teacher at her school and therefore must know everything that went on. I had what can only be described as a mild panic attack. But I decided to focus on positives like Friday night. I asked myself if Nicole were still with me would she have been going out with an ex-boyfriend on a weekend night and the answer was a resounding no. This made me feel much better. I felt like I had turned a corner. I could think about Nicole and Toby the teacher without drowning in a sea of self-pity. It was a moment of clarity, epiphanic even. I had stopped wallowing and started fighting. Clearly I was now ready to win her back.

So I called Nicole's mobile. The ringing tone stopped, then that clicking noise. Nicole answered.

'Hello.'

'Hi Nicole.'

I didn't say who it was because I wanted to see whether she recognised my voice or not. I was doing the cool shit. An old campaigner. No more Mr See-through.

'Who's that?' She asked, dampening my fires.

'It's me.'

'Who?'

'Sam.'

'Sam who?'

'Smith, Sam Smith, *it's me!*'

'Ha, got you!'

'Hey?'

'You were *so* fooled.'

'That was cruel.'

'Well, you needed knocking down a peg or two after all that Mr Smooth crap on the phone the other day.'

'What do you mean? You loved it.'

'Yeah, yeah, whatever, anyway, what's this; you couldn't wait until tomorrow night to speak to me? My, my, you really are playing it cool aren't you, Sam?'

'All right, all right, it's just a … '

'Confirmation call?'

'Yes.'

'You're so transparent, Smith. I think you're forgetting who you're dealing with here. You're going to have to find a new act, I know this routine backwards.'

'Don't you like it?'

'Stop fishing for compliments.'

'Sorry. Still on for tomorrow then?'

'No, I can't.'

'What?'

'Fooled you again. This is too easy, Sam. Like taking candy from a baby.'

'You've developed quite the acid tongue, Nicole.'

'I've missed you too.'

'Really?'

'I was being sarcastic.'

'I know, but have you?'

'What?'

'Missed me.'

'I don't know.'

'Yes or no?'

'Maybe.'

'Have you?'

'Yes. Now bugger off, I'm supposed to be on duty.'

I tried not to get my hopes up but it was impossible. Maybe Nicole was right, all those months ago. Maybe the time apart had been a good thing, giving us room to breathe, affording us the freedom in which to find our way home. Whatever the case, I was in with a shot for sure, making tomorrow night all the more vital. Donnie's engineered meeting in the department store was fast becoming a mythical stroke of genius. Something felt different. There was a correlation there again, one that had previously gone missing. And I was determined to cherish and nurture it like my life depended on it.

Because, in many ways, it did.

19
Friday: 7:32am

The four of us are sat around the kitchen table drinking tea, munching toast, slurping cereal and laughing. It's a glorious winter's morning and everyone has reason to be chirpy. Connor and Techno were revelling in their new careers, and Donnie was in love with a girl who looks so good people pay large amounts of money to see her smile. And I was awash with excitement at the thought of rekindling my relationship with Nicole. The conversation had snaked in my direction and Techno was trying to get his head round recent events.

'I was under the impression Nicole was seeing some new geezer, some poncy teacher sort, as I recall. No offence.'

Terry was renowned for his plainspoken manner. He'd often say 'no offence' at the back-end of sentences so as to legitimise any poorly concealed insults, the recipient feeling duty-bound to accept. His unerring self-confidence was a weapon he utilized adroitly, steamrolling him over conversations.

'The fact that she's agreed to meet me gives me some hope, Techno. Besides, no-one's really sure how 'together' her and this Toby bloke are.' I found myself doing that annoying thing with my fingers when saying the word 'together', like a kind of visual punctuation. Sometimes it's hard to stop being a teacher after the bell goes. It's hard to switch off from the didactic manner, the non-verbal cues and the intolerance of things that are actually quite funny. They all laugh and mock, which I deserve and absorb without argument.

'I bet he's a sneaky two-faced bastard,' offered Techno, optimistically.

'I hope so.'

'You mark my words, Sam. I know the type. He's a try-hard. He ain't man enough to get his own bird so he preys on sensitive, vulnerable ones like your Nicole. She'll see through all that touchy feely crap, you wait and see. Old Techno knows about these things.'

Techno will also refer to himself in the third person. I find it quite appealing. It's like he's been transposed from an old Michael Caine film, always nudging, twitching and winking, giving it the large one, in the know, streetwise. The fact of the matter was that for the majority of the time Techno Terry talked utter shite. But, right at this moment, because he was sticking up for me, buoyant about my chances with Nicole, he was making perfect sense.

'We'll see,' I said, 'I'm not going out without a fight though.'

'That's the spirit Sammy-boy, he who dares wins, my son. Now, how about one more quick cuppa before we scarper? Whose turn is it to brew up, then? Old Techno's a bit parched.'

There's a lot to be said for Techno's outlook. Somewhere along the line he's had an anxiety bypass and now lives life without apprehension or insecurity.

152

He never appears agitated or burdened in any way; he's always positive, extremely self-assured and incontestable. Sometimes he can be a little disconcerting, overbearing and untrustworthy and, in truth, we haven't always sung from the same hymn sheet but on this occasion I gained inspiration from him. Why shouldn't I get Nicole back? Why couldn't I be the better man, the winner? Why couldn't *I* be incontestable?

I got into work around eight twenty, a little earlier than usual, and headed straight for the main staff room. I was sick of the English Office and wanted to socialize with people who, like me, had no interest in Chaucer. I went directly for the kettle. The train had been particularly overcrowded and I was in dire need of caffeine. I'd hoped that by making a drink before entering the main lounge I'd be able to avoid the stress of an astronomical tea round, one that included everyone from the Headmaster to Mavis the cleaner, but somewhere between the kettle clicking and the outpouring of steam my cover was blown. The door to the communal kitchen opened and Paddy's mug burst into view.

'You wouldn't be going solo there would you, Smithy?'

'Me? No way, and, quite frankly, I'm hurt that you would suggest such a thing.'

'But there's only one cup.'

'Seemingly, yes, but I was actually searching for your special mug.'

'I haven't got a special mug.'

'Well, there you go then. That's why I couldn't find it.'

'What?'

'White with three?'

'You got it, Sam. Oh and Callard wants coffee, tea for Johnno, and Frank and Louis want hot chocolates due to the unseasonable cold.'

'Bollocks.'

As I entered the lounge I was confronted by the usual cacophony - the buzz and hum of computer and copying equipment, the distant beat of a stereo, the clink of cutlery and the range of voices already in. It wasn't easy trying to carry a tray full of hot drinks along with my laptop, rucksack and a packet of shortbread creams lifted from the Science cupboard. We always pilfer from the Science teachers because they're too socially inept to contemplate confrontation. I was under considerable pressure to keep spillages down to a minimum and somehow made it to our corner - alongside the rest of the CGDC - without drowning the biscuits in a shallow pool of spilt beverage.

I feared from the outset that my mind might not be focused entirely on the job at hand today. Instead I was busy counting down the hours before I got to meet up with Nicole. The morning meandered. I called Rory's mum for an update on his progress. She said my advice had been helpful and had asked for Rory to be placed in my form group, which I gladly arranged. My plan was a simple one, namely to get him together with Connor for a bit of a man-to-man. Utilise the old empathy factor, which I hoped might prove beneficial to them both. Personally, I was far too close to Connor and miles away from what Rory was going through, so it seemed the perfect option. Rory felt uncomfortable with the stigma of seeing a counsellor, but already trusted me enough to speak to my friend. Diane agreed, as did Connor, and we were on for this afternoon.

For lunch a few of us went to the sushi bar near the tube station for some teriyaki chicken. I asked Paddy and Mags what they thought my tactics should be regarding Nicole. Mags stressed that candour and sincerity were of paramount importance, which was hardly news. She said I should be myself, listen actively and not push Nicole into a corner, that I should make it in *her* best interest to give everything another go. Paddy, on the other hand, suggested I play it cool and drop a few unsubtle hints about some random girls who have designs on me. He also said I should arrive late and get a couple of people to call my mobile whilst in there, thus making me look popular, desirable and over her. I thanked both for their valuable input and made Paddy promise never to consider moonlighting for the Samaritans.

Just before it was time to go back to work, I felt this sudden urge to carry on walking. I'd experienced this feeling before and it usually occurred at watershed moments in my life. The day my father left home I remember taking a two-hour stroll around our village: down by the riverbank, across the green, the cricket pitch, through dense woodland, around by the church and up the hill where the view stretches on forever, that vast green backdrop, dotted with people, places, lives. A view like that helps me find my place, giving me a sense of perspective. When we lost the baby I put it down to natural law. I didn't fight it. Maybe I should have kicked against its current instead of simply succumbing to authority but I chose to ride over the wave and wait for the next set. It's how I cope, with good news and

155

bad. I walk and I look. I remember taking a nostalgic stroll around my old primary school at the end of my final summer before uni started. I had this overwhelming desire to re-visit the shelter of my youth. I stood by gates once so high and a field once so vast and felt the warm autumn sun on my ageing, stretching skin. I guess my aim was to breathe the security and take it with me on my journey. My life is littered with similar rambles, times when I digressed, trying to catch a glimpse of myself in the world, looking for answers. The moment I realised how much I wanted to be a father was during an early evening stroll along an Australian beach. As the orange sun melted into the Indian Ocean I stepped lightly through it's foamy shoreline, inhaling some of its endless composure, finding the space in my heart for my unborn child. That space eventually turned into a void, but I was ready nevertheless. And when Nicole and I split up I could do no more than march alongside the Thames and see where it took me. I hugged that river for miles. I found no answers but, looking back, saw the flow of a mighty river, a river that had forged one of the greatest cities in the world and I realised that time was the essential ingredient.

It was around 1pm, I had a free next so stayed out and walked a little. Our school sits at the edge of a bustling west London suburb; there's enough here to warrant a cluster of young Japanese tourists looking on excitedly as their friend is sketched by a street artist in front of the station. An office worker sits on a crowded bench, eating her pre-packaged sandwich, pigeons flapping, hopping and nodding beside her. An energetic busker croons manfully at passers-by while an elderly couple sit in appropriate silence, sipping cappuccinos outside a bright red cafe. The faces I see are mostly animate, each one invigorated by the colour that surrounds them. Hands in my pockets, standing still, I imbibe the complex air of humanity, of diversity, and I look forward to seeing Nicole later. I look forward to the future. I wasn't sure if I was psyching myself up or calming myself down.

Whatever it was, I liked it and it helped.

20
Friday: 4:30pm

I was still at school after arranging this case conference with Rory, his mother and Connor. There wasn't much for me to do except introduce everybody, facilitate the discussion and throw in a few focus questions. History and emotion would hopefully do the rest.

It was good of Connor to come and I appreciated it. He'd never found it easy to talk about the death of his father and I wasn't sure what was going to happen. As it turned out, it all went swimmingly. Connor was on great form, articulate, informative, candid and empathetic. Rory opened up, poured himself out and certainly felt better for the session. Connor gave little away in terms of personal anecdote, instead choosing to talk of common emotion, which proved the ideal foil for Rory's rawness. Their gratitude was a tad overwhelming but lent me an unmentionable glow for the drive home. On the way back Connor imparted some more good news, that Nasty Nigel had unexpectedly resigned from the video store, leaving Kathy as manager with an option to buy him out. It was all a bit late for Connor but Kathy was thrilled. As a result, so too was Con. I got the impression he was moving faster than normal in terms of cementing their romance, at this rate they could be dating by next Christmas.

I figured being fifteen minutes early was the ideal time to get to Scooters. That way I'd be guaranteed first in and thus able to choose the setting. I was after some romantic lighting in the corner of the pub, away from the toilets, any rowdy drunks and good-looking blokes. I could have a few nerve-settling gulps of lager and work on my tactics: what greeting to use, what topic of conversation to open up with, what level of compliment to throw in, etc. Plus, there was no chance of me being sloshed on Nicole's arrival, a few inhibitions are vital; slurring, fawning, spitting, smelling and tripping aren't, especially when trying to tempt back the object of your affection.

I enter the pub and immediately spot Marco/Mark. He sees me, turns his back and starts drying a wine glass. Fortunately, being Friday night there's another person working; a young girl, possibly a student, with red hair and a bright smile. I order a bottle of lager from her and take my place at a small table for two in the far left corner. There's a single red carnation sitting in a small white china vase in the middle of the table. I look forward to its romantic symbolism coming into play later, and hope it doesn't look out of place. Next to that sits a small wooden stand with a laminated menu stuck in it. I move it to one side as it's obscuring the view to the empty chair opposite. I didn't want anything getting between us. Not tonight.

I take out my phone and call Kathy to congratulate her on the promotion. Meanwhile Marco/Mark is hovering around my table, wiping it half-heartedly and generally being a nuisance. He thrusts the menu back into the middle of the table, avoiding eye contact. I rise above his petty non-verbals and concentrate on the phone call. But I can't help a little indirect wind-up. I pretend I'm on the phone to another love interest; chirping perkily, laying on the charm as he shuffles and grunts back to the bar. Who's the Casanova now?

It turns out Connor hasn't told me the full story with regards to Nigel the Video Nasty. Apparently he'd been involved in some ruck, got beaten up and left the city with his tail between his legs. He was always a bit iffy, I thought. Couldn't have happened to a nicer bloke. Kathy reckoned he'd built up quite a list of enemies over the years. I didn't realise the video trade was so dodgy. Gangsters everywhere, these days. For a fleeting second I wondered if Connor may have roughed him up but then I remembered that Connor wasn't actually capable of beating an egg at the moment, let alone running some second-rate crook out of London.

I figured Nicole would be fashionably late so took out my fresh copy of the London Evening Standard and, as usual, browsed through it from back to front. And just as I was reading about the possibility of a highly rated Italian striker joining Chelsea for an obscene amount of money I heard my name being called. It was earlier than I'd anticipated and therefore threw me a little. I was annoyed with myself. Despite all my preparations she had caught me off guard.

As I lifted my eye-line beyond the top of the newspaper I saw her, standing there in front of me. She was visibly upset, on the verge of tears, and she was breathing heavily, like she'd run here. Her face looked older than I remember, more weathered, heavy with tension, and her eyes contained something different, something that resembled fear. And although her face was still very attractive, the lack of make-up revealed worry lines, a complexion that lacked the verve I had previously been drawn to. She was wearing a long black leather coat, wrapped so tightly around her slender frame I could see the bumps of her clenched fists deep inside her pockets. Her shoulders were hunched, presumably because of the cold outside, and she was wearing a thick red scarf that obscured the bottom of her face; a face slightly gaunt, like a ghost.

She *was* a ghost.

A ghost from my past.

But it wasn't Nicole.

It was Jodie Taylor.

I had only seen her twice before but she was already capable of triggering all manner of commotion inside me, most of which was based around horror and mistrust. I had good reason to feel this way. She was the sister of some of the most feared mobsters in London; she was also at the centre of one of the worst nights of my life. And now she was standing in front of me, a look of dread in her eye, just minutes before I was supposed to be meeting my ex-girlfriend with the sole intention of losing the 'ex' bit.

'Are you okay?' I asked.

'Sam, thank God I caught you.'

'What's up? How did you know where to find me?'

'I got your address off Connor and the other guy told me you were here.'

'Donnie?'

'Yes. But I didn't want to tell him because I don't know how close he is to Connor. I just know that

Connor respects you so much that he wouldn't be angry with me if I told you. God, I'm rambling. Listen I haven't got long to explain everything.'

She *was* rambling. And I was confused. All the while she spoke I checked for Nicole. I knew that Jodie was here for a reason, probably a very good one, but, as yet, she hadn't been able to take my attention away from the door and from Nicole.

But she soon did.

'Slow down Jodie, and tell me what this is all about. Sit down here and explain what you mean about Connor; what's happened?'

I pushed out the chair opposite and she sat down. That chair was reserved for Nicole but something told me that she would never sit there.

Jodie sat down and my heart sank.

Then she continued. 'Sorry, I'm not making any sense, I know, but we haven't got much time and if we don't do something quickly then someone's going to get hurt.'

'Okay, where's Connor?'

'At the Factory.'

'What's that?'

'Sorry, the Factory is the name of the house that my brothers use as a base in west London.'

'*Your brothers?* What the hell have they got to do with Connor?'

'He works for them.'

'What?'

'It's true; he didn't want you to know.'

'But he works for some drug company.'

'That's true, too. But it isn't a legitimate one.'

'*What?* What's going on, Jodie?'

162

I stopped looking for Nicole and started looking up at the heavens in utter disbelief. My hands covered my face as if trying to protect myself from the inevitable bad news I was about to hear. I really didn't need this. Not now.

She explained. 'My brothers offered Connor anything he wanted as payback for getting between the O'Donnells and me. He said he wanted a job so they gave him one. I feel terrible, it's all my fault.'

'Connor works for the Taylors? Doing what?'

'He runs errands, nothing too heavy; until tonight that is.'

'Why; what's tonight?'

'There's going to be a fight. With the O'Donnells. He's out of his league, Sam. He's way out of his league.'

'Let's go.'

I launched out of my seat and wrenched my jacket from the back of the chair. Then I stopped. I remembered why I was there, why I was sitting in that chair, opposite the door, in my best shirt, with the rose and the empty chair and the clear view.

'Hang on,' I said.

'What?'

'I'm meeting someone.'

'So?'

'It's important.'

'So is your friend's life.'

'I know, I know.'

I sat down slowly, all at sea, unsure of where the chair was. Jodie sat too. She leaned over and placed her hands on top of mine. They were cold and bony. With a whisper she spoke, straight into my ear, right into my head. 'He might not be so lucky this time.'

'Hi Sam.'

It was Nicole.

Her voice was startling against Jodie's whisper. My head shot up towards her and I swiftly removed my hand from under Jodie's. And as I did so I knocked over the little white vase. The flower slid out and a trickle of water escaped, dripping over the edge of the table and onto the wooden floor below. It wasn't a good look. Any of it.

Nicole was just standing there. She was holding a bottle of lager in one hand and a glass of white wine in the other; a look of bewilderment was plastered like a billboard over her beautiful face. She had every right to look that way. Here was I, sitting but two inches from another woman, her hands clasping mine, whilst she whispered intensely into my ear. And there was Nicole, wide open, ready to talk.

It was never supposed to happen this way.

But what choice did I have?

'I'm so sorry Nicole but I have to go.'

'What?'

'It's a bit complicated and I haven't got time to explain but … '

'What, you're just going to leave, without an explanation, with her?'

'Okay, I'll explain.'

'I tell you what, don't bother. I've just realised, I haven't got the energy for this. I thought I had, but I haven't. I've just had to listen to that slimy jerk behind the bar go on about how you're always in here with different girls. I only wanted a glass of wine, to get you

164

a beer in. Instead I get all this crap about you and other girls and phone calls. I don't even know why I bothered. It's just embarrassing.'

'Wait a minute, Nic. For a start that bloke hates me.'

'He's lying?'

'No, but … '

'You know what Sam, I don't care. What's the point? I realised that this was the moment to bound in with a match-saving sentence, one that included the words trouble, Connor, gangsters and death. But I didn't. I was too wound up. She'd been stood at that bar, watching me, listening, *believing* whatever that arsehole of a barman had served up between greeting her and pouring a drink. Meanwhile Connor was up to his neck and I was being primed as his only hope and saviour. The stubbornness was like glue, setting quick against the brittleness of our flagging bond.

What I said was stupid.

And as the words flew out, so did the lack of common sense, like vomit.

'Well, it's not as if we're on a date or anything.'

'No, Sam, it's not. I just didn't see you as the type of bloke who'd flaunt his wears in front of me like this. That's all.'

All I could muster in reply was barely worth saying.

'Nicole, I'm sorry, Connor needs me.'

But she'd already turned around and walked out of the pub. I really wasn't ready for her to leave. It wasn't like her to storm out. But the evidence was stacked against me, and stacked against us. She was sad and angry, again. And I wasn't able to comfort her, again. The story was so familiar it made me feel sick. The reasons and circumstances were different but Nicole was leaving and she was upset.

The feeling was the same.

I told Jodie to wait where she was and I dashed after Nicole. But as I got up Jodie grabbed my arm and pulled me back. Her grip was tight and it startled me.

'What are you doing?' I said angrily.

'There's no time.'

'What?'

'Let her go.'

'*No.*'

I was getting tired of being grabbed without good reason. So I shrugged her off and I stormed out of the pub myself. I pushed open the door. Nicole was stepping onto a bus at the end of the street. The queue was probably long enough for me to get on myself but I chose not to. It just wasn't possible. If I got on the bus, the consequences were potentially unbearable. I'm not suggesting I could save Connor's life or even that Connor's life needed saving but considering the information I had, the risk was far too big to take. Instead I stood there in the dark and watched the red double-decker slowly exit the bus shelter and slope off into the dead of night. The feeling of loneliness that assaulted me was unbearable. I unleashed a gasp of anguish and turned myself around. I was filled with the kind of blinkered rage that was fitting for a man about to enter a battle. It was the type of anger that lived on the edge of tears, bubbling, boiling, squeezing out in search of direction. I wasn't scared. I had been scared of only one thing in my life and that was losing hope. And as that bus slid away so that sense of hope moved with it. My fear had turned into hostility.

I walked back into the bar and told Jodie to take me to this Factory. She asked who the girl was but I ignored her question. I was determined not to drag Nicole down any further by connecting her with this chaos, this mess. I had waited so long for that opportunity, that moment. I had dreamed of the day we met again, when the time was right, when the space was right.

I pushed the door to leave, then stopped. The bogus barman was making a beeline for me. 'Wot iz dis?' he bleated. 'Haz it all gorn 'orribly wrong for yoo, met? Datz a real shem, eh?' And with that he laughed.

And I snapped.

I turned round, leant over the bar, grabbed him by the collar and dragged him towards me.

'What iz yoo do-in?'

'Sorting you out, pal. That's what I'm *do-in*.'

And with that I punched him, a firm, well-timed right fist that landed flush on the left cheekbone. He dropped to the floor, clutching his face.

'Right, that's it, your barred.'

'Whatever, Mark.'

Jodie didn't even flinch. She'd seen a lot better punches than that in her time.

I felt like I could take them all on, like I had nothing else to lose. And I wasn't about to let my best friend go, too. As Jodie drove, I made her tell me everything. 'My brothers have arranged a meeting with the O'Donnells, supposedly to clear the air before someone does something stupid.'

'So this meeting is a bluff, right?'

'Yes, my brothers are going to jump the O'Donnells. They've got everyone who works for them ready to ambush them when they arrive.'

167

'Including Connor?'

'Yep, they said he didn't have to get involved but he wanted to.'

'The bloody idiot; he's just taken one good kicking; his ribs are still broken. What's he playing at?'

'God knows, Sam. It's like he's got something to prove.'

'So where's this Factory?'

'About two miles from here.'

'I thought your lot stuck to East London.'

'They've expanded; apparently there's a lot more money to be had over here. I moved here to get away from it all. My brothers used to visit me and realised there was a lot of business opportunities and spare cash round this way, what with all the students.'

'You mean opportunity to sell drugs?'

'Yes, amongst other stuff, but Connor isn't involved in any of that. He looks after Tony and Mick; they really like him; he makes them laugh and that isn't an easy thing to do.'

'No offence, but why do you care?'

'I feel responsible, Sam. Connor's a lovely guy, too good for this. He took a beating for me, it's only right I should at least try and return the favour.'

'He thinks he's a gangster. I can't believe it; it's almost too ridiculous for words. If it weren't so bloody serious I'd probably piss myself laughing. He's watched enough movies, probably thinks he's Robert fucking DeNiro or something. By the way, I don't suppose Techno has anything to do with all this, does he?'

'Techno?'

'Terry Jones?'

'Oh, yes, he's one of their main pushers round here.'

'Did he get Connor involved?'

'He was the one that realised it was Connor who'd got beaten up. He'd heard his name being bandied about and put two and two together. That's how we knew where Connor was. How do you know Terry?'

'From university, I'll kill him when I get hold of him, lying bastard. So this ambush is revenge for that night.'

'Yeah, my brothers see this as their patch and that was the last straw. They've put a lot into this thing tonight and I'm really scared. They were ready to kidnap me, blackmail my brothers. I thought you ought to know. After all, if it wasn't for Connor and you guys…'

'I appreciate you telling me. But if the O'Donnells aren't expecting it then why do your brothers need so many people, why do they need Con?'

'The O'Donnells aren't stupid. They'll still bring everyone they've got, just in case it gets nasty. They don't *need* Connor; he wanted to get involved; he thinks it's glamorous or something. But it isn't Sam; it's anything but glamorous. I'm scared somebody's going to die tonight.'

'So why don't we just call the cops? Connor's done nothing wrong.'

'That's not a great idea; Connor will probably get arrested and if they ever found out you grassed them to the old bill then your life wouldn't be worth living.'

'So what do we do when we get there?'

'We find Connor, then you get him out of there. He'll listen to you. Drag him out before it's too late. I wish I could get my brothers to stop but it's far too late for them; they enjoy it too much. But Connor just enjoys the thought of it. What they do, it's not clever, nothing to be proud of. It's all about drugs and protection rackets and dirty money and loan sharks and beating people up with baseball bats.'

'Is that what they're planning on using tonight?'

'They'll be tooled-up; bats, iron bars, knives, you name it; I wouldn't be surprised if they've got their guns out for this one. My brothers love an excuse to play with their toys.'

We pulled into a secluded car park at the back of a row of industrial warehouses. I'd never seen the place before and felt distinctly lost. Jodie pointed to one of the buildings. It was the Factory, a den of drugs and theft and violence. I told Jodie to wait in the car and I got out. I could hear voices, ghostly noises, intermittent commotion, all coming from the back end of a darkened storehouse that stood towering in front of me. It certainly didn't sound like a mass brawl; there were just a few lingering cries, like the final gusts of a thunderstorm.

I walked towards it. The back door of the warehouse had been bashed off its hinges and there was glass everywhere. Still I felt no fear. I was numb, incautious, almost careless. The remnant noise died suddenly, leaving me with only the crunch of busted glass underfoot and the unhelpful blur of weak lighting to contend with. I squinted, desperate for focus. Then I spotted a lifeless shadow in the corner of the room. It was only partially visible but worried me enough to lure me toward it. A flash of blue distracted me, coming from outside. A police car. There was no noise, just the light. Still I walked, slowly, towards the shadow.

I finally reached it. The shadow turned into a body.

It was Connor.

I was sure of it. I couldn't see his face but I recognised the suit. I recognised the man and I recognised the position he was lying in.

But this time there was no need for an ambulance.

This time there was no pulse.

This time he was dead.

21
Friday: 8:39pm

He was definitely dead.

It's not like I'd seen a great deal of dead bodies in my time, this was my first, but I could just tell. Again, there was blood, even more than before, and it was coming from a wound in his stomach, presumably caused by a knife.

I bent down, sank to my knees, and put my hand on his shoulder. I pulled the heavy mass onto his front. Immediately I gasped. My eyes widened and my mouth fell open. The person was definitely dead.

But it wasn't Connor.

It was Terry, Techno Terry.

I had recognised the suit but not the man. The scene had been so familiar, too familiar. I'd reverted to memory. Fortunately my presumption was wrong. I knew the man who lay dead beside me, my hands covered in his blood, but I was glad it wasn't Connor. I was genuinely relieved; there was a part of me that was genuinely happy, not that Techno was dead but because Connor may yet be alive and well. He may get another chance. And as I looked at Terry I felt no real pity. I was sure in time I would, sure that given the space to ponder this night I would cry for the loss of a young life, of a person I knew, that I liked, who had made me laugh. He would be missed. But I felt nothing of that at the time. I was empty. And, once again, I was facing death with an overriding sense of relief.

I heard the shuffle of footsteps. I half-expected the police to storm in and see me sliding around in the blood of a dead man but some of my good luck had returned. It was Connor, and he was with Jodie.

'Sam, he's dead,' whispered Connor.

'I know, I thought it was you.'

'There's no time now. The police are snooping about at the front. Let's get out of here.'

We sneaked out of the Factory and got into the car. Jodie reversed out and drove away, constantly checking her mirror. Soon we were back on a familiar street.

Connor was first to break the edgy silence. He was on the back seat, next to me, but was talking to Jodie.

'I called the police.'

'When?' said Jodie, baulking at the very mention of the word.

'When it all started; it was mayhem in there. Then I saw Terry on the floor. I had to call, he deserves to be found by someone who won't just chuck him in the river.'

'Did anyone see you call them?'

'No, I went out and used my mobile.'

'What did happen to Terry?'

'I'm not sure, I didn't see. I stayed outside and waited for it all to die down. Once the police got there everyone scarpered. I stayed well out of it. The police haven't found him yet; they were too busy chasing everyone and chucking them into their van. Those voices were coming from a couple of blokes being arrested. We did well to get out of that. I was just about to go home when I saw you in the car.'

Connor looked up at me. He had never looked more innocent or more helpless. Tears fell from his eyes. I placed my hand around the back of his neck. His head sunk into my shoulder and he sobbed, my chin resting tightly on the top of his head. I gripped his shoulder tight.

He was lost and I was lost.

He needed me and I needed him.

Jodie pulled up outside our house; right in front of the doorway that witnessed the initial blows of this conflict. Connor had played at war games, at gangsters, like in the movies but he'd got his fingers burnt, his dreams blown apart. The reality and intensity of this other world had leapt from fantasy and crushed any hopes he had of fulfilment. As we sat in the car, unsure of what to do next, he spoke of the night's events. And he did so with his head down and his eyes shut, as if trying to squeeze the whole mess right out of his system.

'Terry wasn't a very nice person, you know. I mean, he didn't deserve that, but he was bad. He'd changed. This morning I went to see him, to give him a message about tonight. He was outside a school selling drugs to this group of kids who couldn't have been older than fourteen. Afterwards he boasted to me how he's got contacts in almost every high school in the area. He has teenagers selling drugs for him. There was a primary school opposite with these tiny kids running about, the kind of place where Chloe goes, where Nicole works. The bubble burst for me then. I wanted out.'

'So why didn't you just tell them? They gave you the job as a favour.'

'It's not as simple as that, Sam. Once you're in it's different, you're just one of them, no special treatment. I know stuff, not much, but enough, about their operations; about what they buy and sell, I've delivered stuff to half their contacts. It's not easy to get out; god knows how I'm going to do it. They gave me a chance, and they expect me to take it, not bottle out. Besides, they did me another favour.'

'What?'

'I'm not proud of it. But I got a couple of the boys to go and rough Nigel up for me.'

'At the video store? So you *were* involved.'

'I organized it. Tony got a few of the boys together, said it'd be a pleasure.'

'They knocked him about, scared him off?'

'They know what they're doing. A few words, couple of slaps and the promise of more if he doesn't play ball.'

'That's quite funny.'

'I know. Slimy twat had it coming.'

We laughed. And it felt good. Then there was quiet. We breathed and pondered. I lit a cigarette and offered Jodie one. Connor doesn't smoke; it irritates his asthma.

'Do you have to?'

'Don't push it, Con. I thought you'd gone and got yourself killed. Now I need a ciggie.'

'Fair enough, I suppose. You know what though Sam?'

'What?'

175

'I'm glad I bottled it tonight. I'm glad I didn't pass the test. It proves I'm not as sick as them. I've still got some decency left; I'm not like them, you know, not really.'

'We know you're not,' said Jodie, pulling back hard on her cigarette. 'That's why I went to get Sam. I owed you that at least. This morning you said you were looking forward to the fight but you talked about it like you'd talk about going to see a movie or something; you were excited, like a kid.'

'I've acted like a kid. I've really fucked up this time. How the hell do I get out of this, Jodie?'

'Take a few days off. I'll make up something to my brothers so don't worry about them for a while. But they'll want to know what's going on sooner or later. I won't be able to fend them off forever. You know that don't you?'

'Thanks, I appreciate that. And thanks for getting Sam. You've both been great. I could do with a bit of time to get my head sorted. It's all been a bit mental.'

'Will the police be able to trace any of this back to you?'

Jodie answered.

'I doubt it very much; they don't know Connor and he won't be on their records. They're only interested in getting my brothers or the O'Donnells themselves. It's common knowledge that when people die as a result of gangland stuff, the police don't bend over backwards to find the culprits, they just see it as one less piece of scum to worry about; it saves on court time. This is just another turf war to them. In any case, you weren't even involved in the fight. And as for the work you were doing, it wasn't exactly illegal.'

'So who won then?' I inquired, more than slightly interested. I'd wanted to ask for ages but didn't want to be seen legitimising Connor's dodgy choice of vocation.

'From what I could gather, the cops came before anyone could win. They weren't quick enough to save Techno though.'

'How do you feel about that?' I said.

I was worried that the sight of his friend lying dead on the floor had left Connor in some kind of post-traumatic shock. So I asked the question in order to try and get him to open up, before the wound had time to superficially heal over the pain. I'd long suspected that's what had happened after the death of his father. I knew this wasn't in the same league but in many ways I *was* talking about his father. And he knew it. I should have asked before, I knew that now, a long time ago, but it was only recently I'd learnt the importance of talking through your grief. I always had sympathy for Connor, now I had empathy too. We'd both suffered loss but never talked about it, not really. And his was far beyond mine, and buried much deeper. I hadn't had the chance to ask him about his talk with Rory, whether or not it had helped. I'd noticed a lack of emotion, a straightforwardness unbefitting his association, but wasn't sure if it was a good thing or not. I doubted it was. It had never done me any good. And now it all seemed so logical. He knew someone who'd died and needed to talk it through, to ease the pain, to start the process. I could tell by his reaction that he was aware of the heavy load carried by that question. For the first time since getting into the car he lifted his head and looked at me.

'To be honest I still feel a bit numb, Sam. You never really trusted Terry and you were right. At the moment I don't feel anything because I don't like him either, not today anyway. I wouldn't wish what happened to him on my worst enemy but those tears weren't for him. You should have seen him; he'd taken something, some drug, to get him up for the fight. He was acting all weird, all hyped up. His eyes were evil. I didn't even know he was still into drugs, let alone selling them to school kids. I couldn't believe it when he started bragging about it this morning. I had a massive go at him and he threatened to kill me. He was no friend of mine, not at the end. I thought the Factory just dealt with dodgy gear, buying and selling; that's what I was told. They said all the other stuff went down in the East End. Shows what an idiot I am. Once I'd had that row with Techno I just wanted out. But I was trapped, I still am. Those tears were for what I've become. I thought about what I'd been involved with, how I'd dragged myself down. What I'd deemed as ambition, what I thought was me moving up in the world, it was all bullshit, Sam.'

And then Connor said something that confirmed that those tears were indeed for his father.

'All I've done is avoid the truth. I've done nothing right, nothing that would make anyone proud of me. It was never supposed to work out like this. I've lost my way.'

I said nothing, just listened.

'So I'm not going to feel sorry for myself about losing Terry. I hope they catch the bastard that knifed him, but at the end of the day, there'll be no-one selling drugs outside the school gates tomorrow. So don't worry about me on that score, worry about the poor little kids who are now hooked on whatever shit it was that he was flogging them.'

It was time to halve the problem, to be a friend, to be honest.

'Maybe I've let you down, too, Con.'

'How do you mean?'

'I don't know, maybe I should have talked more, talked properly, been there for you, realised you were having a hard time. There's more to being a mate than beer and football.'

'You've got your own stuff to deal with, Sam. Weren't you supposed to be meeting Nicole tonight?'

'Yeah, but I was too busy saving your arse.'

'Sorry, Sam.'

'It's not the end of the world, not yet anyway. By the way, I've been meaning to ask you, what were all those text books about?'

'What?'

'You brought home loads of books about pharmaceutical products, for your pretend new job.'

'I got them from the library; knew they'd fool you.'

'Sly bastard.'

'Piss off.'

'You piss off, you plastic gangster.'

'I've seen stuff that would make your hair curl, mate.'

'Whatever, Con. You were only in the mob five minutes.'

'You don't know the half of it.'

'Neither do you. You were outside, remember?'

'True.'

'Idiot.'

'Prick.'

At this point Jodie started laughing. Connor and I had reverted to kind, without realising. Soon the car was full of a different kind of tears. Despite the bizarre nature of the conversation it was the most normal few moments I'd had with Connor for days. This was because, like so many of our normal conversations, it started off serious and ended up inane. More often than not they end up in the gutter. This one was slightly different. This one dragged us out of the gutter. The laughter, however inappropriate, was our release. When we finally settled back down we knew that our lives were still in a state of mild chaos, a melting pot of grief and monotony, treading that line between reinvention and a constant craving for the past. But the tears in our eyes were proof positive that, at our very fabric, we were still okay and we were still together.

As we said farewell to Jodie and strolled into the flat I had a strangely optimistic feeling, a feeling that there was a way out. I didn't know what the way out entailed but I could see a glimmer of light at the end of what had been a dark, nightmarish tunnel.

As it happened, it was Donnie who provided that way out.

First of all though, someone had to fill him in on the night's events.

22
Friday: 9:23pm

'Connor's a gangster. He works for the Taylors. Earlier on tonight there was a huge gangland fight between the Taylors and the O'Donnells and Techno, who also works for the Taylors, got killed. He was a drug dealer for them. Jodie Taylor came and told me about Connor so I went to try and stop him from getting involved. As it happens, he didn't get involved and he called the police. Now they're all over the scene like a rash. Oh, and I missed out on my date with Nicole. She now hates me but that's not the main issue here. I did get to punch out the smarmy barman, which felt good. But Connor's kind of tied into this gangster lifestyle thing now. You're not really allowed to leave once you know stuff, apparently. Jodie's going to stall them but we need a plan. Why are you laughing, Donnie?'

'Because you're taking the piss, right?'

I was trying to explain the night's events to Donnie. He was sitting in one of the armchairs in our living room wearing a fluffy white dressing gown and very little else. One of his hands was clutching the remote control while the other was scratching away inside his Calvin Klein's. I really wanted to ask him to stop fiddling with himself but didn't want to waver from the importance of the real issue. It took a fair while to persuade him these stories of gangsters, drugs and murder were legitimate. And as I relayed them I even found myself questioning the validity of it all. If I hadn't actually been there, I would have presumed it a pack of lies.

Understandably, his reaction was one of disbelief. Initially he tried to get his head around the fact that Techno Terry 'had been wasted' (his words). Once that sunk in he tried to get to grips with the idea of Connor being involved in 'some heavy shit' (again: his, not mine). Then he took issue with Connor for 'lying his arse off' (same thing). Then he pondered the fact that Techno was a 'no-good dealer' (and again) and finally he reflected upon the sad notion that I'm 'unlucky as fuck' (ditto) when it comes to getting back together, or not, with Nicole.

It was a tough conversation to endure for several reasons. For a start, Connor had to sit there and go through another guilt trip. Again, I was left pondering what might have been as regards Nicole. Plus, we were all knackered and, not least, Donnie spent the whole time playing with himself.

Donnie, being Donnie, didn't huff and puff about it; he didn't lose control or get overly sympathetic or tearful or patronizing or judgmental. He simply sat there, turned the TV off, took his hand out of his boxer shorts, looked at Connor, looked at me, and said, in the broadest Aussie twang I'd heard since our early days, 'Bit of a bugger all round really.'

He rubbed his forehead - with the same hand, as it happens, though I didn't mention it, didn't seem like the right time - before getting up and walking to the kitchen. Connor and I stared at each other, curious as to what he was going to do or say next. As a pair we'd hit a roadblock. Now we needed something from Donnie. It was a big call, but we had faith in him. First we heard the kettle boil, then the familiar chink of mugs being taken from the mug tree, then the sound of three separate pours, the fridge open and shut and the high-pitch clink of a stirring spoon. It wouldn't take Sherlock Holmes to work out exactly what he was doing but it was strange the way he moved, the way he looked. You could almost hear the intensity of his thoughts. He hadn't forgotten us. Quite the contrary.

He eventually re-entered the lounge carrying three mugs of tea, without the need of a tray; his oversized rugby hands clearly up to the task. He made a non-verbal gesture that consisted of two sharp nods of the head. We translated this as meaning 'sit down fellas, I've got something to say'. So we did. And we were right; he did have something to say. And it was good, too.

'Okay, I've got an idea,' he started, defiantly. 'Actually, I've got two ideas but I'm only going to tell you about one of them. The other I'm going to work on myself while you two are carrying out the first. And, if the second part comes off, it'll sort everything out nicely. But there's no point getting your hopes up, it may not happen.'

At this point I was hoping that the brilliance of Donnie's plan did not lay in its rationalization. I hoped that beneath all the awkward presentation lay something we could at least understand.

I needn't have worried.

'I'm sorry if this is all a bit cryptic but that's the way it's got to be if I'm going to help get you out of this mess. Right then, the way I see it we've got two major problems: letting the dust settle on tonight and then getting the Taylors off your back for keeps. First things first, Connor. I suggest, and it's only a suggestion, that you bugger off back to Ireland for a day or two. The reasons for this suggestion are as follows: firstly, you'll be out of the country; secondly you'll be somewhere familiar; thirdly, it's cheap to get there and, last but not least, you keep saying how you'd like to go back and visit the old place, so here's your chance. It would only be for a couple of days, staying one night, but it's the change of scene you need right now. Okay, Sam, I strongly advise you go with him. You can hold his hand and maybe sort a few things out of your own. With that in mind I suggest you try and persuade Nicole to go too. You two obviously need some time to talk and this is an ideal opportunity. I expect she's sick of you putting your mates first, so here's a chance to look out for Connor as well as say your piece to her. Don't leave it too long without explaining everything and don't give up, not now. Get her a ticket, book into a nice hotel and show her a good time. Connor can visit a few rellies and you and Nicole can re-light the fire. A weekend away will do you all the world of good and when you get back on Sunday night I'll hopefully have sorted out the second part of the plan; namely to get the Taylors off your back. What do you say, boys?'

We were stunned. The plan was good, and explained so nicely, in the end. Well, it was good save for one small detail. How the hell was I supposed to persuade Nicole to come with us? Meanwhile Connor was

184

hugging Donnie. By the look on Donnie's face the gesture was somewhat unnecessary. Donnie, like all men, loves a man hug, but there's protocol to adhere to: a time limit, a reliance on alcohol, a preference for manly patting as opposed to girly squeezing. Connor appeared to be breaking every rule in the book. He eventually let go, leaving Donnie to deal with the awkwardness of it all. He then grabbed my laptop and booked three tickets via the Internet for the following morning, leaving from Heathrow at ten thirty. It had all been arranged within half an hour of Donnie's opportune brainwave.

Meanwhile I skulled a large brandy, shivered under the density of alcohol, picked up my jacket and headed off to Nicole's place.

I was praying for a minor miracle.

23
Friday: 10:10pm

I knew that if I got the chance to explain the situation properly to Nicole she would understand. Whether or not that meant flying off with me to Dublin the next day was highly debatable, but I had to try. Getting the time to speak was the key. Regardless of whether she'd be buying into Donnie's plan, I had to talk to her about my behaviour in Scooters.

I reached her block of flats and looked up at the window of her bedroom. I saw her shadow glide across, behind the drawn curtains. I knew she was there. I pressed the buzzer and waited. Nothing. I pressed again, long enough to show my intent but not so long so as to annoy anyone. I heard footsteps coming down the stairs. It was Sara, her flatmate, best friend and, by the look on her face, confidant and bodyguard. She opened the door aggressively. I've witnessed people close a door with aggression, but never open one with such ferocity. This was a first. I could sense an outburst coming. And I was right.

'I'm sorry Sam but Nicole doesn't want to see you. She came back in a hell of a state after she met you. She told me what happened. I don't think you realise how much she was looking forward to seeing you. She was really excited, and then to see you with another girl, well, that just broke her, and all that stuff about other girlfriends and phone calls … What were you trying to prove? It's none of my business, I know, and you don't owe me an explanation, but what the hell were you playing at? Couldn't you have waited for a time when you *weren't* meeting Nicole to hold some tart's hand and whisper sweet nothings into her ear hole? Or was it just some sick plan? I never picked you as the type, shows how much I know. And what the hell are you grinning at?'

It was true. I was smiling. And if that didn't sufficiently antagonise her I proceeded to completely disregard her question to ask one of my own. The thing was, I just had to pick up on something she'd said, the bit about Nicole *really looking forward to it.* I knew I was innocent. I'd just forgotten I'd already been proven guilty.

'She was *really* looking forward to it, you say?'

'*What?* Yes, but I don't know why you're grinning. You've totally blown it. She doesn't even want to see you, let alone listen to you drivel on about how sorry you are about being a no-good womaniser.'

Maybe the smile and the question were inappropriate but the news was great. Well, potentially it was great. It was utterly useless if I didn't get to speak with Nicole. I couldn't help labouring the point with Sara, despite her obvious disdain for my manner.

'So do you think she wanted to get back together, then?'

'Are you *mental*?

'No, I just … '

187

'Are you drunk, is that it? Because I don't seem to be getting what is essentially a very clear message across to you, Sam. For the last time, yes, she had extremely high hopes for this evening. But you seem to have misjudged Nicole somewhat. She was kind of hoping to *not* see you all over some slapper. Call her old-fashioned if you like, but she was actually hoping she'd find you on your own, both emotionally and physically, and not all over some other woman five minutes after you were supposed to be meeting her. And then to hear from the barman that you're some kind of Casanova, always in there with other girls, or talking to them on the phone, trading slobbery banter, it's just *so* not like you. And while we're on the subject, your new friend Marco, he's a wanker. Treated me like shit. The bastard. You deserve each other. He's not even really Mediterranean, you know, he's from bloody Brixton. He's a fake, just like you.'

Time for the big guns.

'I was scared that Connor was about to get himself killed.'

'What?'

'He's been involved in some really dangerous stuff, Sara. That's what that girl was telling me. I had to go to save Connor from getting himself hurt, or even worse. I had no choice.'

'Are you for real? Because if this is another one of your ... '

'Honest. I swear. Listen, do you remember Terry Jones from uni?'

'Techno?'

'Yes.'

'Of course, very dodgy geezer if you ask me, cute though; why, what's he got to do with all this?'

'He died earlier tonight, as a result of being involved in the fight that I was trying to get Connor out of.'

'Seriously?'

I nodded.

'I see; shit, this is all a bit heavy. Has this got anything to do with that fight last weekend?'

'Yes, but I'd appreciate it if you kept it to yourself.'

'Okay.'

'So you see, there wasn't anything going on, I wanted nothing more than a night out with Nicole. I'm devastated it all went wrong.'

'You'd better come in.'

'Oh, and Sara … '

'Yeah?'

'The girl on the phone, it was Kathy, Connor's girlfriend. And, as for Marco, he's not my friend, I hate him. He was twisting everything around, to get back at me. I punched him last night, after Nicole left.'

'Nice one. Look, I'm sorry if … '

'That's cool, Sara. You were just looking out for Nic, looking out for a mate.'

'So were you by the sound of it.'

'Guess so, don't feel much like a hero, right now though.'

'The thing is … '

'Yes?'

'Well, it's not really me you've got to convince.'

'No.'

I stood in the hallway, dry-mouthed, waiting for Sara to explain all this ridiculousness to Nicole. They were in her bedroom, door closed. I could hear their muffled voices but couldn't tell what was being said. Eventually Sara came out and said to go in. It was a room I'd been in hundreds of times before but this time I felt like a stranger.

Nicole was sitting on her bed in her dressing gown. The room looked different; re-decorated, rearranged. There were no posters on the wall, just a couple of framed prints, and the bed had been moved round to another corner.

She looked strong enough, on the surface. But she didn't look happy. And I needed her to be both. I was clinging onto the tenuous notion that I could, given time, make her happy again; that it was life, not me, that kept letting her down. But for the first time I felt like a hindrance, that I was no good for her, that me being there was detrimental to her long-term happiness. Yet I stayed. I stayed because I'm weak, because I clearly want what's best for me above what's best for her. She looked weary, like the anger had been beaten up by fatigue. Her face showed all the signs of a spirit that had been gnawed at, energy-sapped. Beneath the strength of her stare she was vulnerable. I couldn't help feeling like I was going in for the kill, willing to trample over every nerve just to get a stab at completion. Was it for the good of me? Yes. Nicole? I don't know. I doubt there's a lawyer in the land who could convince a jury that I was good for this girl right now.

'Hi.'

'Hi Sam; sorry I'm in such a state.'

'No, Nic; I'm sorry you're in such a state. It's all my fault and if I was any sort of a man I'd leave you now, walk out of here and let you get on with your life.'

'But you're not going to, are you?'

She smiled, half a smile.

'No; if it's okay with you I'd like to sit here, explain what happened and then I've got a proposition for you.'

'Bear in mind I'm not going to be all that receptive. Whatever your reasons for tonight, however valid, I'm still upset, I'm still hurt and I'm still very tired.'

'Okay.'

So I sat there, perched uncomfortably at the end of a bed I used to call my own. Half of that bed was mine; it was referred to as 'my side'. My watch used to live on the bedside table alongside my glass of water, ready to quench my night-time thirst. I recounted the story of the evening so far and, as I explained my actions, Nicole appeared to visibly thaw. She accepted my explanation and was a little freaked out by the intensity of it all. Again, the talk of gangsters, turf wars, drug dealing and the death of an old university friend all sounded highly implausible. But it was true. And I was being honest. I sat there in silence and let the words sink in, computed by a girl who deserved more than life had thrown her way. I felt neither awkward nor comfortable, just somewhere in between.

She accepted my need to leave the pub to go after Connor. She was wary of that stubborn streak, she'd suffered from it before and I could tell it was hindering my cause. But I was talking now, which spelt some kind of progress. Every time Jodie or Abby's name was mentioned she'd screw her face up a little, which I liked. She admitted to seeing red upon her arrival, what with all the hands and the whispering. She also accepted that her storm-out policy might have been a little rash and out of character. Looking back, I liked it, but I didn't say. She said she wasn't proud of acting like an extra from an American soap and yes, she had been looking forward to the evening, very much. I regretted the hurt. We really didn't need it. What I didn't regret were the types of emotion she was admitting to feeling. All were akin to mine, which was good news. Suddenly I didn't feel so horrible. Nicole was still strong and I was still in the game.

Well, I *was*.

Until I blew it, again.

Nicole refused to come to Dublin. And I'm afraid this frustrated me. I know it shouldn't have, I know I should have expected such a reaction and I know that even though I felt discouraged I shouldn't have shown it, but I did. I didn't actually say it. I didn't have to, it was written all over my dim-witted face, leaking into my body language. Technically I was just upset but the incredulous events of the recent past had mugged my sense of reason. Feeling upset was starting to look awfully like being frustrated, annoyed even. Nicole saw it and she was angry.

'I can't believe that you thought I'd say yes. I can't believe you're so damn sure of yourself you assume I'd drop everything and go away on some dirty weekend with a man who, a couple of hours ago, made me feel so sad I cried my eyes out. I haven't cried like that since, well, you know the last time I cried like that because I was with you then as well. In fact, I only ever seem to cry when I'm with you.'

'I'm sorry. I just thought it would be a good chance for me to make it up to you. That way we wouldn't have to linger on tonight and we'd get the chance to talk properly, to get away, to discuss whatever it was we were going to discuss tonight. You never know, we might have fun.'

'Yes, I suppose it would clear your conscience.'

'It's not about that.'

'You sure about that?'

'Okay, fine, I would like to make it up to you. I do feel guilty. I never wanted any of this. All I wanted was for us to get back on track, to start again, to try again. That's all I've ever wanted. Do you think I'd rather see dead drug dealers than spend time with you?'

'You wouldn't have had to see any dead drug dealers if you'd stayed with me.'

'I thought you said you understood why I had to leave?'

'I did, but then you annoyed me.'

'You wouldn't expect me to ignore what was going on, would you? You know I couldn't just disregard something as serious as that?'

'Well, sometimes I think that's exactly how you treated the loss of our baby.'

That last sentence came from nowhere and it fairly struck me down, right between the eyes. It really hurt. I don't think that that was its intention but it hurt nevertheless. It hurt because Nicole truly believed it. If it'd been said to simply get a reaction then it would have been easier to take, a spiteful jab said in the heat of an argument. But it wasn't. Nicole said it whilst looking straight at me, she said it with a calm voice and she said it with tears rolling down her face.

Yet more tears.

A nervous silence followed. There was no way I was going to speak. I wanted the silence to eat away at her.

'I'm sorry Sam, I didn't mean it.'

'That's okay, but you did mean it.'

'I didn't mean it to come out like that.'

'It's what you were thinking though, wasn't it?'

'I wasn't thinking straight.'

'I'm glad you said it. I'm glad because I'd rather you were straight with me. I hate it when we censor our feelings.'

'I thought it but I don't believe it, not really.'

'What *do* you believe Nicole? Tell me, please, because I don't think I've ever really asked you. I know I should have done but I haven't.'

'I don't know.'

'Tell me, please.'

'I think that when I lost the baby … No, Sam, this is too hard, I can't do this now.'

'It can't be any harder than all the other stuff, the pain, the suffering, having our lives torn apart through no fault of our own. Maybe the time *is* right. Maybe it's finally time to hammer it out.'

'I wanted to talk a long time ago.'

'But?'

'But you acted like talking about it was wrong, like we were living in the past, like we needed to forget about it. I didn't want to forget about it.'

'I know that.'

'You do?'

'Yes, I do *now*, but I didn't then.'

'So what's changed?'

'I've had time to think; I needed to think first. I just didn't seem able to talk.'

'You were so busy making out that it didn't affect you in the same way it affected me that you made me feel guilty for letting it affect me at all. You alienated me.'

'I was just trying to cope, same as you.'

'But you weren't trying to cope *with* me, Sam. You were trying to drag me through it quicker than I was ready. In the end I had to get away so I could sort my head out without being shoved into a corner. I had to get away.'

'So did I.'

'So what does that say about us?'

'That we know what's best for us. We know our limitations, our needs, even if it doesn't seem like we do at the time.'

'Do you really believe that?'

'Yes, and I believe in us. I've got a huge problem with some of the crap that's been thrown at us but I still believe in us. Yes, we lost a baby and it killed me but I still had you, I still had hope, whereas you didn't seem to have any. And we may not cope with things in the same way or take the same amount of time over things but that's because we're different people. I think we got so close that we expected to react the same to everything, including the miscarriage. I was just glad to have you.'

'So glad that you didn't care that we'd lost the baby?'

'Did I look like I didn't care?'

'No.'

'Exactly; I just figured that if one of us didn't try and pick us up as a couple then we'd be down in the dumps forever. I admit that was wrong but doesn't the fact that I thought it was the right thing to do mean anything?'

'Of course it does but it doesn't change the fact that we should have stayed together. You should have waited for me.'

'I know.'

'I wanted you to stay with me.'

'But the time and space has got us here, talking.'

'It should never have come to this, Sam.'

'But it has, and what do you want now?'

'Peace, Sam; I just want peace.'

So I left her in peace. I gathered my shattered ego and wandered home. I felt like I'd given everything but come away with nothing. And that was worse than not knowing.

Because I had no hope.

Which is no excuse for what I did next.

Two hours later, I was in bed, drunk, with Abby North.

Putting the past to bed.

Quite literally.

24
Friday: 10:49pm

Two hours before going to bed with Abby North, I skulked back to the flat and threw my keys on the table. They made a tremendous crash. I looked at them, pondered their symbolism and wondered how my life had spiralled out of control.

When I was a kid I didn't own any keys, I simply didn't need them; there was always someone at home, I was never alone. Then I got a small key for the lock on my bike. It wasn't much but signified ownership and required me to memorise a code of numbers, the first signs of responsibility. Then, when I hit my teens, I was given a solitary door key for those few occasions when I was home alone. They then began to pile up with monotonous regularity: car keys, house keys, window keys, work keys, dad's house, mum's house. There were just too many, weighing me down, turning me into some kind of medieval dungeon master.

I'd emptied my pockets. There were too many of them, they were too heavy and that's why I threw them. In my world, responsibility seems to precede maturity. It sneaks up, nagging me to do the next thing, before I've mastered the last. I wished I could have said the

197

right thing to Nicole. I knew now that she had been ready to make a go of things and, despite being armed with that knowledge, I still couldn't deliver the right words in the right order.

I went into the lounge. I could hear Donnie on the phone in his room so I knocked on Connor's door, hoping he was in the mood for some company. I didn't much feel like talking but didn't feel like being on my own either. He shouted for me to come in so I opened the door and sat on the end of his bed. He was sprawled along it, his head perched against a pile of pillows. He had one hand behind his head and the remote control for his stereo in the other. He turned the music down and looked up at me.

'Didn't go too well then?'

'You could say that.'

'She's not coming?'

'No.'

'Sorry Sam.'

'Don't worry about it. How are you feeling?'

'Pretty good really, excited about tomorrow.'

'Any word on what the other half of the plan is?'

'No, he's been playing it cool, been on the phone for ages but I can't make out who he's talking to.'

We discussed the night's events: Nicole, Connor's short-lived sortie into gang warfare, our imminent trip to Ireland, the size of Abby North's breasts, and more besides.

Then Connor dropped a bombshell.

He told me something new about himself, something that threw me, shocking me momentarily.

And he said it like he was confessing to the most heinous crime.

'I've never been to my father's grave. I've seen it from a distance. I know exactly where it is in the cemetery, I know what it says, off by heart. But I've never been able to walk up to it, you know, read it. I've never been able to stand by it, to just be there. And I feel ashamed about that. But I'm going to do it, tomorrow. I'm going to visit the grave of my father. And knowing that makes me happy; it makes me look forward, Sam.'

The fact he'd shared that with me meant he was, indeed, moving forward. That he was right when he said he was ready. It made me feel proud, like we were moving forward together. He was a picture of calm and assurance. A heavily built secret had been raised from his slender frame. He was ready to enjoy life without the strain, without the weight.

He carried on.

'I couldn't face the funeral, Sam. At the time I didn't realise how close the funeral was to the actual death. I thought I had ages to sort myself out. I guess at that age I'd never really thought about it before. I wasn't ready. I wasn't ready to see my father being buried in the ground at the bottom of the hill, the same hill we raced up together, by the sea where we fished, the beach we played soccer on. I didn't understand that the funeral was part of the process, that it would help me sort myself out. So I guess I never really went through that grieving process. I never realised the importance of it, you know. I'm still suffering now. I wasn't ready emotionally, not until now anyway. I tried, you must believe me, I tried so damn hard, standing at that gate. It's sounds stupid but I knew that if I did see the stone, then he'd definitely be dead, because it was written down and all. I used to daydream about him coming back one day, saying that the cancer was a bad one but he went to a special doctor in London or New York who knew how to fix it. Reading, on the stone, the year he died, would have stopped that being possible. I knew deep down, but, hope, you know, is something.'

'Reminds me of how Nicole was.'

'After the miscarriage?'

'Yeah. That was the scariest bit for me. It was like she'd lost all sense of purpose, of living, of having a future.'

'Sometimes the future's just too scary, especially when you can't even cope with the present.'

'That thing you said about the funeral. We didn't get to have one either. That's how Nicole must have felt, too. I can see that now, now it's too late. There was no ceremony, no send off, no celebration, no release. So it all just turned inwards on her, you know.'

'*Is* it too late for you two?'

'I think it might be.'

'That's a shame. You're going to fight for her though, right?

'I don't know if I've got any fight left, Con. I'm not sure I had that much in the first place. It's funny, my dad used to say that it's not about the size of the dog in the fight but the size of the fight in the dog. I used to love that saying. He used to say it about bullies at school or bigger kids in rugby. It made a lot of sense back then.'

'It still does. My dad used to stay stuff like that. Stuff that keeps making more sense as you get older.'

'I feel bad. My dad's alive and well and I'm not even talking to him, well, unless you count discussing his delinquent stepson.'

'I thought you liked the kid.'

'I do. Which is even more annoying.'

'You're just a whingeing git, Sam Smith, so you are.'

He exaggerated an Irish accent that, until that moment, had been slowly melting away. I know that this scared him, like he was losing his past.

'Seems like I've been falling out with everyone lately,' I said, full to the brim with self-pity.

'My advice, Sam, for what it's worth, is that you don't leave it too long, with either of them. You never know what's around the corner. The way I see it, I was lucky. I had the best father. I would've loved more time, a lifetime with him, but it wasn't to be. But he was the best. I'm going to see him tomorrow and he's going to help me through all this. Sort yourself out, Sam. Don't let the past haunt you, hinder your future. Life does that enough anyway, without tempting fate. That's what I'm going to do, sort myself out, so I am.'

A sense of wellbeing, of strength, descended over Connor. It hailed from somewhere way beyond the confines of the room, filling his chest.

'For so many years now I've been trying to pick myself up and get myself ready to do it. The ironic thing is that it wasn't until I reach my lowest point that it finally feels right. I always imagined going back over there when I was rich and happy and together, so that Dad could be proud of me. But I'm actually going to do it because I *need* my dad, not because I want to show off or anything. I need his inspiration, time with him. I need to go there to grow up. It's the next best thing to getting a clip round the ear or a pat on the back from him.'

'It's great that your dad can do this for you now.'

'It is, I feel good about that.'

'I'm excited about seeing your home town. How far is it from Dublin?'

'Howth? About nine miles up the coast; we'll get the train. I'm going to surprise a few people. It's beautiful there, right by the sea, and there's a few cracking boozers too. There's quite a bit of money there these days. When Dad's business took off he moved us out of Dublin and into this lovely big old house right at the top of the Hill of Howth. You can see for miles. He grew up there as a boy; wanted me to enjoy the same sort of childhood, with all that fresh air and goodness, kind of wholesome, you know. It was a great place to be, back then.'

'Sounds awesome, especially that bit about the pubs. It's just a shame I couldn't share it with Nicole, really.'

'Give it time, Sam.'

'I've tried that, thought time was the answer, but it's not.'

Donnie was still talking away on the phone when I decided to call it a night. It had been a pretty forgettable day all round. Fortunately I was too exhausted to worry into the night. Just before putting on my headphones for a spot of self-indulgence, my mobile rang. It was Abby, wondering how the date went. I told her. Ouch, she said. She offered to take me out for a quick nightcap somewhere. Why not, I thought.

This time I insisted on the Fox and Hounds. Once I'd called Large Barry and confirmed my suspicion: that he couldn't go two weekends without a lock-in, I phoned

Abby back and changed the venue from a trendy, ambient late-night wine bar to outmoded local with damp. I'd tried going up-market, bettering myself, being the new man, and failed miserably. Again, I was late to meet Abby. This time she wasn't propped at the bar tapping someone up. There was no chance of that in here; she will be treated like a !eper until the locals deem otherwise. It's nice to have a system one can rely on. When I finally arrive she is sitting alone in the corner, nursing a glass of wine that, alongside her face, projects a slightly awkward shade of red.

'Bit crap in 'ere, innit?' she barks.

'The Fox? Crap? Go wash your mouth out girl.'

'Everyone keeps looking at me funny.'

'Really?'

'Yeah, that fat bloke behind the bar spent the whole time staring at my boobs and breathing heavy.'

'You're just paranoid, Abs.'

'And those two playing pool. How scary are they?'

'Well, I'll have to agree with you there. Misery Morris is slightly mental but Monkey's a pussycat.'

'Monkey's a pussycat!'

'Yes.'

'What is this place, a pub or a zoo?'

'Bit of both, I suppose. How's your wine? Nice drop?'

'Tastes like warm piss.'

'Right.'

'Didn't work out with Nicole then?'

'Could say that. Bit of a disaster as it happens.'

'Nevermind.'

'Easier said, than done.'

'Sam.'

'What?'

'That bloke's staring at me.'

'Where?'

'By the fruit machine. He keeps sticking his tongue out and winking.'

'Don't worry, that's just Greek Tony. Top bloke, when you get to know him.'

It was hard. Trying to justify my local to an outsider. In fact, it was nigh on impossible. Like that phrase: *you had to be there*. Well, you do. You do have to be there, to truly get it. Three times a week for six years. Then you get it. But I didn't have the energy. Abby's whingeing was annoying me. She was a foreigner and she was diluting its appeal. So, after necking a couple of quick pints I said my farewells and frogmarched her back to the flat.

We got in, opened a bottle of vino, threw on a bit of *Coldplay* and fell into the sofa. She wanted sex. It was obvious, even to a man who owns absolutely no radar equipment at all. It was up to me - a quite ridiculous amount of pressure to bestow upon a man who was, emotionally, in a dangerous place, even before the acquisition of alcohol.

If this was a watershed, then what better way to start over? It's how I began adulthood, with Abby on top of me, bouncing away. And now, here she was again, my ticket to the future, to futile revenge.

We walk into my bedroom.

Posters adorn the wall. Boyhood stars wink at me as I pass. Ian Botham: the arrogant swashbuckler. Now I lie beneath him. Abby soon follows. I think about kissing her. It will be a weird, wonderful, passionate clash of tongues. Still no guilt. Just revenge. And proof. Proof that my life is a fluid, roadblock-free ride, unfettered in its hedonistic fixation.

'Nicole's loss is my gain,' she offers as we lie opposite each other.

'What?'

'I'm glad I never gave you enough to get Nicole back.'

'I don't understand?'

'Well, I wasn't exactly overflowing with ideas, was I? I wanted a piece of you for myself. I saw you first. You're mine now, Sam. Who needs relationships anyway?' She leans towards me, eyes shut, mouth open.

'Hang on.'

'Hey?'

'I can't do this.'

'What?'

'I'm sorry. I don't know what I was thinking. Things are a bit messed up at the moment. This isn't what I want. It's all wrong.'

With that, she gets up and heads for the door. I stop her, worried about the time of night, her mood, my conscience.

'Don't go, Abby. It's late, stay here, it doesn't have to be a big drama.'

'I feel a bit stupid though, Sam.'

'I'm sorry.'

'I hate being second best. You know me, always was a bit too competitive.'

But there was no competition. I realise that now. I say nothing. Instead I shoot Abby a friendly smile, grab a blanket from the wardrobe and head for the sofa. And although I'm only moments from sleep, I've never felt so awake in my life.

25
Saturday: 7:52am

The night zooms past and soon it is morning. There's a blanket of drizzle covering the street beneath the kitchen window but I have no intention of letting it dampen what is a very important day for Connor. It's a trip I'm determined to see through. This time I will not be running ahead. I will be sticking by his side, letting him dictate the pace. It is a journey that will, hopefully, end in resolution, reconciliation, a meeting of sorts. I once failed to complete a similar journey alongside Nicole. It too followed the death of a loved one. My attempt to disturb the cycle of life in mid-flow failed. I'd since learnt that you couldn't manipulate the passing of time. It's hard to learn your lessons late, but vital nonetheless. The key to that future seemed one key too many for me at the time. Connor felt he was strong enough to endure this and I admired him for his self-appreciation and his courage. It had taken a great deal of time for him to reach this place. I just wish I had shown the same patience in the face of loss.

I looked in on Abby. She was fast asleep. She looked sweet, and I appreciated her investment in me. She looked like a friend, a good one, potentially. I left her and went for a shower. Then I packed a bag, ordered a taxi and ate my breakfast. Meanwhile Connor was moving about the flat slowly, silently. Donnie was still giving little away with regards the second part of his plan, though he did say everything was taking shape. It would all be revealed upon our return. I didn't tell the boys about Abby. I figured she'd be well gone by the time Donnie was back from rugby.

Ten minutes later we heard the beep of a horn and the rumble of a stationary engine. I peered out the window. It was veiled in mist. I wiped it clean with the sleeve of my jumper, clearing the view with a couple of squeaky rubs. Tiny balls of water clung to the wool, refusing to disperse.

There's something friendly about the chug and rattle of a London cab; all shiny black, with its smooth, affable lines and its brilliant orange light. He was ten minutes early so I sent Connor outside to ask him to hang on a minute whilst I finished my cuppa. I watched Connor dawdle out, shoulders hunched, hands in pockets, walking slowly towards the cabby's window. I felt a stab of helplessness, like today is too big for him, and for me, like we've grown out of our skins too quickly, too early, before the new ones are ready.

He leans in.

The back door opens.

And out steps Nicole.

I look, compute, then feel strong, then weak, then strong again. All within a fraction of a second.

She's carrying a bag, wearing a smile. She hugs Connor. I fumble the window open and call down.

'NICOLE!'

Her eyes lift, squinting in the falling drizzle. She calls back. 'I thought I should make the effort, seeing as you asked so nicely.'

Unbelievable, especially after last night.

Then it hits me.

Last night.

Abby North is lying in my bed.

Nicole is walking into my flat.

26
Saturday: 8:30am

Honesty had plummeted down my list of priorities. The truth just didn't look that good right now.

I ran into my room. Abby was fast asleep. I snatched my bag, ran over to Nicole and picked her up. I was genuinely ecstatic, if a little annoyed that I couldn't truly savour the moment without fretting. This was my punishment, not being able to fully appreciate the magnitude of our reunion. Still, plenty of time for that, let's just get the hell out first. I grabbed Connor's bag, before fairly shoving the two of them out the door, insisting we wait for our cab outside. I needed a cigarette anyway.

'So what made you change your mind?'
We were sitting in the back of the taxi, a bizarre air surrounding us. Nicole leans in, touches my hand and whispers gently, 'Because I love you.' These words are like a springboard, a giant leap into the future. She places her head on my shoulder and we enjoy the silence. There was plenty to thrash out, plenty of unfolding and decoding to do, but, following all the

noise of the recent past, this was both blissful and necessary.

It was what we were used to.

Connor was unnaturally quiet. No wisecracks, no banter, no drivel. And this continued throughout the flight, spending much of his time staring out into the vast cold blue of the ocean. Then, at the start of our descent, his face lit up as the green of his homeland rolled into view. He was buzzing inside. I was glad to be there, beside him, ready to drag him up and dust him down where necessary.

In contrast to Connor's thoughtful pose Nicole and I enjoyed a fairly animated journey. We started with a few apologies before launching bravely into the miscarriage. It was cards on the table time. I acknowledged trying to fast-track her recovery, she confessed to shutting me out. We both agreed that the time and space apart had, eventually, facilitated our recovery. It really didn't matter if this were all true or not, what mattered was we were making similar noises, trying, together. There was a sense of picking up where we'd left off. We'd never been angry at each other, just angry in ourselves. Now we were forging our fears, designing our future around them. We agreed, no relationship should be judged on its darkest hour.

Nicole explained her change of mind in regard to the weekend away. It wasn't that she didn't want to, nor that she thought it a bad idea. The dirty weekend jibe was a smokescreen, a retort. She was slamming on the brakes, didn't want me dictating the pace again. But this time she was unwilling to negate my positivity, not when my only motivation was to lift us off the canvas, to get us fighting again. There was one more issue that was nagging away at me however, standing between the next bout and the last drubbing. And it revolved around a certain work colleague of Nicole's. Toby the teacher. Surely even he wasn't so trendy as to sanction a trip like this?

'So, are we together, then?' I asked, with an intensity and bravery that struck me as highly improbable.

'We were never really apart, were we?'

'We weren't *together*.'

'No, not physically perhaps, but we hadn't let go either, had we? We hadn't really moved on in that sense.'

'No, well, *I* hadn't but … '

'But what, Smith?'

'I thought you had.'

It flew out, and had no right to do so. Had it gone through the proper channels, it would have been refused entry. But the vetting system had malfunctioned and I was left with the level of censorship more befitting the Swedish Arts Council than a highly sensitive post-break-up conversation with Nicole.

I'd figured she was far from besotted with him but that was no longer enough. I wanted written proof he was of no emotional or sexual relevance, that he was somewhere between a civil acquaintance and a shoulder to cry on. And, seemingly, I was unable to wait for such evidence. But I'd unwillingly re-entered the verbal comfort zone, gate-crashing to the next level. After feeling the warmth of the past, I'd lulled myself into thinking I was back there. Trouble was, there would never have been a subject as spiky as Toby the teacher back then. I had fallen between two stools. And it now appeared that one or both of those stools was about to hit the fan.

'*What do you mean*?'

'Oh, nothing.'

'No, come on.'

'It's nothing, forget it. Look at the view, it's simply stunning.'

'Sam.'

'Yes.'

'What about honesty? We're not going to get very far if we don't tell each other the truth.'

'Well, it's just that I was under the impression you were sort of seeing someone.'

'*What?*'

'It's okay, I'm not mad.'

'No, but I bloody am; who am I supposed to be seeing?'

'Toby the teacher.'

There, I said it. Now I was left wondering whether or not to go and take cover in the tiny toilet at the back of the plane. Asking that question was like throwing a grenade. It had been gnawing at the back of my mind, like a barrier between the present and future. Now I was about to be furnished with the real truth, either that or get beaten up, thus ending the shortest reconciliation in romantic history.

The level of noise that eventually hit did turn heads. Prior to that, there had been disbelief, of my manner, and maybe my insight. Then I sensed this ascension of pressure. I could just make out Connor, squirming, in the corner of my eye. After all, he'd blown the whistle, uncovering their sordid little affair. If I was going down, I'd be dragging his sorry arse with me.

Then she exploded.

She exploded in squeals and howls of laughter.

Connor and I looked at each other. We were relieved but mightily confused. Had I unhinged her? Were these the evil cackles of a psychopath? Was she on the edge of a loathsome revenge? When the cackling finally died, she peered up and, between the tears and the exhaling, said, '*Toby?* Toby's gay. You've got more chance of shagging him than I have.'

I struggled for words.

'Right. That's good to know, well, not the shagging bit, not that I'm in anyway disgusted by that, not at all, you know, my brother's, well, that's just good, sorry to er, good, yes, nice. Did I mention the view?'

'I'm presuming someone you know saw me with him, right?'

At this point Connor threw me one of those ferocious little headshakes, his sole intention to completely disassociate himself from the conversation. Nicole carried on, unaware of Connor's manic non-verbals. 'Toby and his boyfriend recently split and I was trying to cheer him up. He's a good laugh but not really my type, being gay and all.'

'So who *is* your type then?'

My efforts to both change the subject and fish for an undeserved compliment were shameless I know but, as it turned out, well worthwhile.

'You are, you idiot. Anyone who can make me laugh like that has got to be worth hooking up with.'

It wasn't much of a compliment.

But it was more than enough for me.

27
Saturday: 11:48am

We landed at Dublin airport. Compared to the long haul flight to Australia it was no more than a coffee break between London and Ireland. I patted Connor on the back and held Nicole's hand. She gave me a squeeze, an injection of strength. I wished it could've been reassigned to Connor; he looked like he could use it. He'd suddenly turned a weird shade of nuclear green that had little to do with aviation sickness. There was nothing we could do, it was all part of the process.

We took a taxi into Dublin and tasted the vibrancy of a city balancing old and new with ease and grace. We did the whole tourist thing while Connor psyched himself up. First we jumped on an open-top bus that circumnavigated the city at an agreeable pace. We stopped off only once, at the Guinness factory, before boarding the D.A.R.T train for the short journey to Howth, Connor's former home and resting place of his father. As the train shuffled unhurriedly between stops Connor slowly took control, proving an excellent host and tour guide. By the time we reached our final destination I felt quite spoilt by his attention to detail. The green post and telephone boxes took a bit of getting used to but the overwhelming sense of conviviality amongst the locals was like fresh air to us all. Their good nature reminded me of the residents of Australia, never moving too fast for a greeting, never too burdened for a yarn. It was a good place; I could feel it. You could really sort your life out here, I thought.

Connor's knowledge of Howth was immense. As we walked out of the station and imbibed the beauty of its peninsula, we started to realise why his passion for this part of the world still burned like a beacon, making sense of whom he was. He explained how the village was studded with historical significance, built by an army of brave fishermen alongside those who'd fled the hustle and bustle of Dublin. He recreated its majestic past, how its origins stretched right back to the Stone Age, talking of megalithic tombs, Celtic forts, Christian oratories, Viking ramparts and Norman castles. Nicole and I were dizzy with knowledge, our minds racing along with the enthusiasm of a local boy.

He told us how his grandfather used to drive the trams, how his uncles fished for a living and how he and his friends would climb the hill, enjoying long summer adventures. He recounted the times when his father ferried across to Wales on business. He and his brothers would gather gorse and sticks and light a bonfire at the top of that hill so his dad could see it as he sailed out of Dublin Bay.

It was the place he tuned his senses, where his imagination ran free amongst the natural beauty, unhindered by the modern and the new. He pointed out a small but beautifully formed island, exquisitely named Ireland's Eye, that sits out to sea, the most captivating natural backdrop you could wish for.

And then there was the Abbey where the grave of Connor's father lay waiting. The wondrous old ruins of St Mary's stands dramatically, precariously, on the edge of a cliff overlooking the harbour below. As Connor stood by those ancient ruins, he too hovered uncertainly, between the sea and the graveyard, between life and death. But he did not, could not, enter, instead insisting on showing us around the village properly before entering that small, intimate cemetery. By the way his hand was shaking uncontrollably as it clung to the black wrought iron gate that separated the living from the deceased, I'd say he was buying a little time. No one was going to push him before he was ready.

We walked up the Hill of Howth, ingesting the colour along the way. Tiny rows of crooked houses lined our path; the quaintest of shops selling trinkets and all variety of craft; and the odd pub, built on the stories of regulars. Old men sat out on street corners, outside their homes. Some were alone, contemplating quietly, others in pairs, putting the world to rights, each of them happy to spare the time to smile, nod or tip the peak of flat caps, each one representing a brick of harmony and clarity in a village that felt closer to nature and closer to your own heartbeat, and the heartbeat of others. It was the perfect place to catch up, for us and for Connor.

Once we'd taken in the views of Dublin Bay we ventured back down the Hill of Howth. We had worked up quite an appetite so decided to have lunch in a pub near the station. It was there that, after a generous helping of steak and ale pie, Connor informed us of his intention to go back to the Abbey. The tension immediately heightened. I tried to release some by suggesting he was just trying to get out of paying his slice of the bill. But it was clear that this was no joke. It was also clear that if he didn't grasp the opportunity whilst his levels of enthusiasm and commitment were hovering just above acceptable it was likely he'd go home unhappy and unfulfilled, feeling worse about himself than ever.

I offered to escort him but he politely declined. He stood up to go. We wished him well and arranged to meet on the east pier whenever he was ready. He went out the door only to re-enter two minutes later.

'Actually, guys, would you mind coming with me to the gate?'

We agreed to do whatever it took. He didn't want to do it on his own but he still *really* wanted to do it on his own. It was heartbreaking to see but we all knew it was the kind of pain that was necessary.

As we reached the gate I half expected him to turn and run. I wouldn't have blamed him if he had. But he was determined not to reduce the importance of the situation with anything remotely resembling cowardice. Connor wanted this done properly, like he'd been through it in his head a thousand times; there was a sense of ritual about his movement. It was a solitary ceremony, bereft of pomp or pageantry but there was protocol and there was solemnity.

He opened the black wrought iron gate and carefully shut it behind him.

He would be on his own until he reached his father.

We watched as he moved, slowly, towards one of the many gravestones that sat up at various angles in this cramped but peaceful spot. The lively sea beyond offered strength. He stopped and stood, head bowed, staring longingly at a single white stone. It was weathered but well maintained, touched by nature and human hand alike. He knelt down, reached into the inside pocket of his coat, pulled out a short solitary flower and placed it by the foot of the stone. He talked soft, inaudible words, and tears fell from his eyes. They were good tears, in their way. They signified breakthrough, a meeting of hearts.

Nicole and I walked away, leaving Connor alone with his thoughts, his memories and his father.

We strolled along the pier, mostly in silence, save for the sea.

Half an hour later we returned.

Engaged to be married.

28
Saturday: 4:13pm

It wasn't something I'd planned to do, not there, not then. Having said that, it was fortunate I'd grabbed the box back at the flat because the moment cried out for the gesture.

Seeing Nicole step out of that taxi had re-ignited me, turning all the hope into something real. I'd ran up to my bedroom to check on Abby and, just before closing the door, looked over at my chest of drawers. I opened the third one down and fumbled around, well aware of time, and of Nicole's presence. At the back of that drawer, amongst all the T-shirts, socks and boxer shorts, was that little box, the one with the ring inside. I picked it up and put it in my bag. Realistically I didn't see myself asking that question; the one I nearly asked all those months ago. I was just too scared of reaching the moment without it.

As we walked along the pier, hand in hand, with the bracing winter wind swirling about us, we talked a little of Connor and of us. Of how far we'd come, where we'd been, the cyclic nature of it all; and suddenly I had an overwhelming urge to cement the moment. It was ridiculous really; again I was pushing her, we were hardly back on speaking terms, it was Connor's day and we were still beholden to a faction of underhand villains. Apart from all that, it was perfect. Besides, I was sick of trying to squeeze into my own life, with all its routines and responsibilities, its unwritten laws, its protocol, its time management, its risk assessment, its best practise strategies, its necessity for female friends and fashionable pubs.

She said yes.

So who cares.

Standing at the end of the pier, we held tight and looked over towards Ireland's Eye. I could feel the power and the volume of the waves belting the rock beneath us. I could feel the importance of the situation. The sea was playing for us. It crashed, boomed and sprayed like an orchestra in the fullest of flows.

It was all the backdrop I needed.

The courage I felt came from nature; it was working with me on this one, which I appreciated. I pulled out the box and opened it. Nicole looked down and up and then down again. Her hands cupped her mouth, as if to shut out all the anxiety and apprehension. The diamond was there to help me, and it too came from nature. It focused, quietened her. She was ready to hear me out, and that's all I asked for: a little more time and a little more space. And for the first time in a long time I said exactly what I wanted to say in the way I wanted to say it, and at the right time.

'I'd planned to do this once before. This is a different country, a different time and a different ocean but it's the same ring, they're the same feelings and it's the same thing I want. So, Nicole, will you marry me?'

'Yes.'

I was a little surprised to be honest. Let's face it, she didn't even want to come to Ireland with me in the first place; she'd even been in two minds whether or not to go for a drink the other night. But I was being honest about my feelings and I was being honest about my intentions and I think all that helped. It didn't feel like we were rushing anything, not really; it actually felt like unfinished business, better late than never. We'd managed to come a long way in a short time. This after coming a short way in what felt like a very long time. There was symmetry there. It felt right. And it also felt right to see Nicole wearing a stone from the fertile earth of Australia. We shared a self-congratulatory embrace and I kissed my fiancé for the first time. The symbolism of the ring was matched by the fact that it would be good old Connor who we would tell first.

We saw his languid walk come into view at the other end of the pier and I commented to Nicole that although he didn't know it yet, there was our best man. But first things first, this was Connor's moment. He was the protagonist. Ours was merely an upbeat subplot, a positive respite supporting the real drama. We had no intention of stealing his thunder so we agreed to wait until the time was right to tell him, however far in the future that might be.

He walked and he walked, the full length of the pier. We didn't know if he was walking the road to salvation or walking the plank. All we knew was that he was walking towards us, slowly but surely, just like he always does. And he got to us in the end. He stopped, looked up and spoke quietly, hardly audible against the thump of wave on rock. But we heard what he said. In terms of its message, we heard it loud and clear.

'I'm desperate for a pint, anyone else fancy one?'

It was fair enough that after such a traumatic experience Connor would appreciate a quick injection of alcohol. His nerves probably needed calming, but it didn't stop us from laughing. We'd waited for him to reach us for what seemed like an eternity and the tension had slowly built. We wondered how he'd be coping, how he felt, what he'd say. What he did say was typical of the man: unpredictable, strangely logical and extremely funny.

So we found another pub. Connor said it was a particularly good one and we were in no position to argue. What he failed to mention was that this one was owned and run by his aunt and uncle. As we pushed open the front door there was a brief moment of recognition and then a huge roar of acknowledgment. He seemed to know everyone in there and soon they all knew us too. Or at least that's how it felt. Connor's Auntie Margaret and Uncle Michael grabbed us all with equal fervour and, for a minute there, I wondered if they all knew about the engagement. When I realised that was impossible I wondered what kind of reception a piece of news like that would get around these parts. Amongst all the furore I got out my wallet and Connor laughed, 'You won't be needing that in here, mate.'

It was a warm place, an extension of a family home, like the way pubs should be, the way homes should be. After attending to the important business of the day Connor started to enjoy himself. He hadn't wanted to see any family until he'd been to see his father. Once done, it was time to celebrate. It was the wake he'd never attended. He got there in the end. We all got there in the end. After a couple of swift ones he began to unlock, one by one, unbuttoning his feelings. He was proud of himself, of his dad, of the times they'd shared.

'It just felt right,' he said on reflection, which in itself meant it was worth the pain.

Being fairly typical of our gender, it would have taken a lifetime for Connor to clock the ring on Nicole's left hand, so I went to the bar and ordered a bottle of champers to nudge the process along. I also insisted on paying for it, which wasn't easy. I took the bottle over to our table, now consisting of six others joined together, and I raised a glass to our best man. Connor calculated the statement, then stood up and cheered. His toast was a simple one: 'About fucking time.' Swearing doesn't seem to be a huge issue round these parts.

We were celebrating on two fronts, Connor's return home and our engagement - not that these guys needed an excuse for a party, the fact that it was Saturday would have been ample, I'm sure. And as late afternoon bled into evening the party gathered momentum. The log fire burned and crackled whilst one of Connor's uncles played a mesmerizing, foot-tapping fiddle, while we clapped alongside our new best friends. It was a fitting end to a big old day. We called home with our news. Donnie seemed genuinely moved, sad not to be part of it, happy to have initiated proceedings. The plan was complete, apparently. I looked forward to the fanfare and finale.

Connor had yet to mention the Taylors. He didn't want to drag the occasion down to their level, tarnish the good name of his father. He did, though, raise a glass to Techno Terry, making his peace. Connor's auntie wept with happiness on hearing the news that her nephew had finally visited the grave of her brother. It had obviously been cause for concern within the family.

I felt small amongst all the good will and posthumous concord. Connor's father was still dead. Mine was alive and well, bumbling about with his teenage stepson. Yet still I couldn't find a place for him. But, strangely, I felt closer to him now, over here, closer than I had for some time. The blend of booze, music and merriment was soothing for us all. Nicole and I danced and clapped and rose to the occasion. And once he was suitably composed, slouched amongst cousins and uncles, Connor began spouting tales of gangland Britain, of rescuing broads and taking on the big boys. The prodigal son had returned, and he was clearly enjoying the limelight.

Nicole grabbed my hand and dragged me over to the bar. We sat on stools, our knees rubbing, talking loudly into each other's ears, struggling to be heard above the continuous fiddle diddle. Unsurprisingly, the conversation slid toward the gutter. It'd been a long time between drinks, so to speak. I was first to dip my toe, finding the temperature somewhat balmy.

'I've *really* missed you,' I slurred.

'Oh yeah, how much?'

'Well, old Donnie's permanently on the nest, even Connor's getting some these days. I think its about time I filled *my* boots.'

'Jealous, were we?'

'Of Donnie? No way, he may be a pulling legend but he's never had what I've got.'

'No way, not again.'

Now that didn't sound right.

I got the distinct impression Nicole had misheard me, thinking I'd asked a question, when I hadn't. Between her lips and my ears, amongst the thick colourful cloud of strings and voices, something had slipped, like a gas, and was suddenly pluming between us. And not even the numbing blur of alcohol could be blamed. Nicole kept talking but I didn't hear a word. Instead I steamed in, cutting her down, determined to rewind.

'What do you mean, *no way, not again*?'

'Nothing, I mean I'd never, you know, I want you, I'm *with you* now.'

'There you go again, what do you mean *now*?'

'Shit.'

'Right, let's go outside.'

So we went outside. I lit up a cigarette and inhaled deeply. Nicole walked in front of me, stopped at a wooden fence and faced the ocean. Orange lights flickered weakly in the distance beyond. The white light of a faraway lighthouse exploded every few seconds. The cold was sobering, the feeling familiar. Nicole turned, blonde ponytail swaying as she moved. She had that Buffy look again: thick, fitted polar neck jumper, blue faded jeans over knee-high black boots. The same boots I'd been fantasising about unzipping with my teeth just minutes earlier had, suddenly, kicked me right in the guts. Leaning on the fence; the one that neatly frames the pub, Nicole explained exactly what it was I'd stumbled upon; information I was never meant to have.

She told me how she'd had sex with Donnie.

29
Saturday: 10:20pm

The numbness I felt certainly had something to do with the cold, maybe something else to do with the sharp coastal wind, but mostly it was born of disbelief.

'We weren't together, you know, you and me. I'd never even met you when it happened.'

'I don't understand.'

'It was at the start of university; we'd bumped into each other a couple of times, got to know each other a bit, went to the same parties; usual story, too much booze, too few inhibitions. Not my normal style, as you well know, but hey, these things happen. He wanted to meet up again but I knew we weren't compatible. I didn't know that *we'd* hook up. When he introduced us …'

'That little lovely.'

'What?'

'That's how he introduced you.'

'Was it?'

'Yes. So why didn't you tell me at the time?'

'Hardly the most awesome chat-up line of all time, *I slept with him last week, do you want a turn next?*'

'Suppose not. But why didn't *he* tell me?'

226

'We thought it best that way. I don't know why he didn't tell you at the start, maybe because he wanted more and I didn't, maybe he wanted to save face, I don't know. All I know is, I'm sorry it came out here, now.'

'Verbal comfort zone.'

'What?'

'You think you're back, but you're not, not quite, and you forget to censor stuff.'

'I guess.'

'It's still weird.'

'I know.'

'Was he … ?'

'*Sam.*'

'Sorry. I don't really want the answer.'

'If it makes you feel any better, I can't even remember. I'd had about twelve vodka and grapefruit juices by then.'

'We used to always drink that stuff, at uni, one with every pint.'

'They tasted great, didn't they?'

'No. I *hated* the stuff.'

'So why drink it?'

'We used to love ordering them.'

'What?'

'We used to love asking for a *V.A.G.*'

'I remember now. You used to go up and say, 'Large vag please?''

'Fantastic stuff.'

'Sammy.'

By now she'd moved in, sensing me thaw a little. She was brushing against my ear, like a cat before breakfast.'

'Yes, Nic.'

'You're the best, you know that. You're *my* little studmuffin.'

'Really?'

'Oh yes, of course.'

'Not Donnie the Don, the Italian stallion, the Aussie surf-dude?'

'Who?'

'And you don't remember *anything*?'

'Nothing at all.'

'I'm going to kill him.'

'Good for you, babe.'

'He's an arsehole.'

'Yes, he is.'

She was purring now.

I had no chance.

I was sure the subject would rear up again, given different company and more alcohol, but for now at least, it was okay. I felt strangely composed, surprised at the level of logic I'd applied to the situation. It had proved a strange revelation at the butt-end of an even stranger week. It had also been a long few months. There seemed little point in turning around and walking straight back down the tunnel now, not when there was that light, that sharp glow of the lighthouse, in the distance.

We woke next morning to the homely sounds of the pub. Like us, it creaked and yawned as we made our way down the carpeted staircase into the huge whitewashed basement-kitchen. We never made it to the B&B we'd booked; it just didn't seem right to leave. Connor's auntie provided a breakfast fit for the Lord of Howth himself, black and white pudding providing welcome variation to the bog-standard fry-up we get back at the greasy spoon on our street. Then we said our farewells and headed back into Dublin for a final wander around before going home.

The flight was a great deal more relaxed on the return leg. This was especially true for Connor who made up for the eerie silence that shrouded him yesterday. Nicole spent much of the flight inspecting her engagement ring. She kept doing that thing that women do with rings, holding up her hand, stretching out her fingers and twiddling the ring with the tip of her thumb. It was good to watch. Connor tried to lower the tone by going on about what a lovely 'ring' Nicole had. Every now and then he'd ask to get a good look at her 'ring' to which he'd add that it's the nicest 'ring' he'd ever seen. It was typical of Connor - find a fairly ordinary joke then hammer it out until everyone's sick of it, then say it some more. It's how he gets a lot of his kicks. Still, it was preferable to getting them by joining an infamous crime family. He was back, I suppose. Plus, I'd be lying if I said I didn't find his childish wit slightly humorous, the first ten times at least. Nicole didn't care either way, it seemed nothing could dampen her spirits. I couldn't believe my luck.

It was getting late by the time the taxi pulled up outside our block of flats. The good news was that Nicole was staying at my place; the bad news was that Connor was still going on about Nicole's 'ring', his incessant innuendo now sinking to new depths. He'd spent the whole cab journey from the airport thinking up new one-liners. There would be a ten-minute gap, then a new *double entendre*, followed by a dirty little chuckle, and another ten minutes of silence while he brewed up an even more tedious effort. There was a part of me that preferred him when he was depressed, at least he was serious then, at least he was quiet.

'So let me get this straight,' he continued, feeding off our lack of energy and interest, 'your finger is currently inside *his* ring?'

As I turned the key to our front door my senses jammed, arresting my movement. Initially, it was the distinct aroma of expensive cigars, then the familiar trill of Al Martino, the guy from the *Godfather* movie, pumping from the stereo. He was singing *Volare*, which could only mean one thing.

And I was right.

There, sitting on our sofa, wearing a smile as big as the ocean was the second and final part of Donnie's plan.

30
Sunday night, 6:26pm

It was Bob, Bob Rossi, Donnie's dad.

He leapt up, flung out his arms and demanded a bear hug all round.

'Who's first then, don't be shy, come and give old Bob a squeeze.'

I knew he was here to help, I wasn't sure how exactly, but from the moment I saw him - the Hollywood tan, the bright white grin and the jingling gold - I knew everything would to be fine. More than that, I knew it would to be fun, too. There's no half-measures with Bob. He has a habit of making things happen, of getting his own way. Underneath the cockney twang, the laugh-a-minute barrow boy exterior with all its twitches and nods, ticks a heart of gold and a fiendish mind. He hadn't come all this way to let anyone down; that was for sure. After the hearty welcome we had a brief catch-up session over a can of lager. Bob held Nicole's hand, told her how proud he was, then slapped me on the back, winking wildly. He turned to Connor, cupped his face, stared and whispered.

'Connor, my son, it's a tricky business and no mistake. But you can rest assured now. I've still got a bit of clout round this manor. It's all sorted. Gutted about your pal, Con, but it's a tough fucking business and you're too good for it. Shit, even I'm too good for it. Straight and narrow, you know it makes sense, boy.'

He bunched his fist and gently patted Connor on the brow, as if knocking the sense back into him. He allowed himself a short laugh, rubbing his face at the same time.

'Cocky little fuckers, those Taylor boys. Always were. They're slack, no respect in the job. It's a different world, these days, gone downhill, so it has. We used to take pride in our city, in ourselves. We'd wear nice clobber, look good, feel good. They've turned the place into some druggy hole; poncing about in poxy tracksuits. I'm glad to be shot, tell you the truth. Used to be about the community, upholding our own justice. These days it's got more to do with the law of the bleedin' jungle. Animals, the lot of 'em. '

Connor looked and listened intently. He'd always loved Bob, with all his larger-than-life stories of East End mobsters. He made it sound so much more right and proper than the grimy existence of those boneheads Connor had been embroiled with. Connor was much more vocal in his support for Bob's infamous past than Donnie ever could be. Donnie tends not to ask. It's not that he's embarrassed or uninterested. It just scares him; after all, it's his blood too. There's a lot to live up to, or get away from, or sit comfortably next to. The way he sees it, his old man was born at the same time as him, re-born if you like. The other stuff is too close for comfort. I knew it couldn't have been easy for Donnie to drag his dad back through the past, thus acknowledging it all himself, to ask him to relive those days, to re-enter the fray. And although I couldn't quite shift that thought of him and Nicole, I softened a little, pushing back the vision, exposing his goodness, the reasons for our friendship. As Bob delved deeper, recounting chronicles of a youthful partnership with the eldest of the Taylor brothers, Donnie interjected, polite, firm, controlled.

'Dad, tell him about the plan.'

'Yeah, sorry son. You know me, old motormouth. Okay, here's what's going on … '

As the plan unraveled, one thing stood firm, permeating from start to finish: Donnie's blinkered determination to save Connor. Following his ill-fated backchat with the O'Donnell mob, Donnie had worked everything out. His relentless push to get his old man to return for one last dip into the underworld – a place Donnie found cold and eminently avoidable – had led to this point. As soon as Connor had dropped the name Danny Taylor back at the hospital, Donnie had a sniff of an angle. He remembered the name from somewhere, from photo albums, anecdotes, an echo from the past, a distant ripple in a vast ocean. His initial hunch was compounded by the story surrounding one of the Taylors being on the board of directors at a London soccer club. That's where he'd heard it. His dad had mentioned Danny Taylor during conversations about football; he was an old beer pal from way back. They grew up together in East London, old school, still kept in touch. But Donnie didn't mention it at the time. He felt it might have encouraged, even legitimised Connor's admiration for such people. Donnie thought that if he explained everything to his dad then he might be able to get Connor off the hook. Bob was a bit long in the tooth for putting the squeeze on people but had the past on his side. He knew the right people.

Bob agreed and immediately set the wheels in motion. He'd arrived from Australia just a couple of hours before we got back and had already been in touch with Danny Taylor who, being the eldest of the brothers, still had quite a hold over the other two despite having retired from the heavy stuff. Like Bob, he was no angel, but drew the line at getting kids hooked on drugs. In his time he was a master of the muscle game: protection, doormen, bodyguards, but never drugs. It's a strange code of conduct, stemming from a time when people had to create their own rules, their own brand of even-handedness.

Danny Taylor agreed to Bob's request and promised to lean on his brothers to free-up Connor. This was strictly on condition the two of them met up the following day to get blind drunk down at a few old haunts. Bob's arm didn't take much twisting. He left Danny to round up a few faces for a good old-fashioned knees-up. You could almost see the tension melt away. Connor was too grateful for words. Instead of trying to verbalise his gratitude he simply grabbed hold of both Bob and Donnie for another one of those earthy man hugs. Bob asked him to mind the shirt, as it was a personal favourite. Then he ordered Donnie to get the Duty Free champagne from the fridge and bring in a few glasses.

We phoned Large Barry and arranged a bit of a shindig of our own, an engagement do, down the Fox and Hounds for tomorrow night. He agreed and, seeing it was us, promised a good spread, no expense spared. He'd even dust off a few complimentary bottles of sparkling wine on condition we didn't tell his missus about the party until after the shops shut. He feared she'd fritter any potential profit on a new frock. We bet him fifty quid he couldn't keep that sort of information from Sandra for twenty-four hours. Easy money. He promised to inform all the locals and gave me his word that, despite the short notice, we'd get priority over any previous bookings. Yeah right. Bob said he'd come to the party straight after his meeting with Danny Taylor. Visibly excited, he admitted it'd been a long time since he'd been to two parties in the one day.

With Bob on the sofa we slept a little easier that night. Especially Connor. I was already sleeping better, due in turn to a different type of security, that of a returning girlfriend. And Nicole echoed those thoughts. I was already over her random night with Donnie. I'd successfully reduced it to an insignificant fumble, laying no malice at either door. But then, through no other reason than the haphazard nature of thought, I stumbled upon an ugly link. Now I knew. I knew why Donnie failed to unveil the details of his most memorable one-night-stand - he was talking about Nicole. Suddenly, it was a given.

I had to confront him.

31
Monday: 8:17am

There's nothing like the brittle rub of cold and the prospect of a week at work to test your mettle when you think you're happy. The downpour that greeted me as I left the flat was a bit uncalled for. I ran for cover in the deli next to the train station, shook myself down like a dog and bought a few treats to make myself feel better. Armed with a tacky morning tabloid, a large latte to go and a fresh blueberry muffin, I sprinted to the relative dry of the station. I joined the queue for tickets and baulked against a whistling wind that was threatening to bypass my skin and head straight for the marrow in my bones.

Everyone at work was delighted with my news. Their positive response made me feel a tad disorientated, yet faintly fuzzy. No doubt they were just relieved that all the browbeating, bellyaching and chin stroking was finally coming to an end. There was even the odd female student who appeared relieved. It's surprising how far you'll travel for a sympathetic ear.

Rory was back at school, keeping his head down and his nose clean. He smiled knowingly as I passed him in one of the myriad corridors that pump students round our campus. The heart of the school felt strong, intact. And I had a good day, extracting and lending knowledge, focusing minds and laughing with students, from the snotty-faced little ones through to the elegant and the worryingly self-conscious at the top of the school; each one preparing themselves the best they can for a world outside those walls; walls that simultaneously protect and frustrate us all.

7:02pm

We were pleasantly surprised on entering the Fox and Hounds. Large Barry had put up a congratulatory banner, which in turn meant he'd actually stood on a chair, or even a stepladder, a huge compliment in itself. Then there was the smorgasbord, meticulously arranged on three trestle tables at the back of the pub; everything from pickled eggs to vegetarian quiche. He'd even remembered my personal favourites: *French Fancies* – the pink and brown ones are the nicest, always get eaten first, leaving the yellow ones feeling moist and unloved. I relayed this to Large Barry who said that the yellow ones sound like his missus. The turnout was equally impressive; especially considering it was a school night. The majority of these guys don't talk about anything that may undermine their tough exteriors. Most of them don't even *think* about their emotions, let alone talk about them. No one ever showed them how and no one ever explained to them the importance of doing so. It's not the way they were brought up; it's not part of the social vocabulary around these parts, especially for the boys. We were touched that so many of them had voted with their feet and come out in support of our engagement. Sandra, naturally, got a new frock for the occasion and with it went any extra profit Barry would have gleaned from such a busy night. But he was still in a good mood, which, again, was a compliment. Or it may have been because I let him off the fifty he owed me. Too soft, that's my trouble.

Nicole was pleased to be back in the fold at The Fox, joking it was the deciding factor in getting back together. In a fit of magnanimity I gave her my brother's mobile number. She felt sure he'd be a perfect match for Toby the teacher. My mind boggled at the thought of it but I handed it over anyway. If I could help my brother out, enable him to feel the way I do right now, then the bizarreness of her matchmaking was a small price to pay. Immediately, number in hand, Nicole left the pub to make the call. Then, without the buffer of my fiancé, I found myself gravitating towards Donnie, who was perched on a stool at the bar. I see this juncture as an excellent opportunity to talk to him about anything other than Nicole. Two sips later, I bring the subject up.

'She told me, you know.'

'What?'

'Nicole; she told me about you and her.'

'Oh.'

'Why didn't you ever mention it?'

'What was the point?'

'Do you two ever talk about it, you know, have a laugh about it?'

'Yeah, all the time, Sam. Sometimes we re-enact it.'

'What?'

'Of course we don't, what do you take me for? What kind of friend do you think I am?'

'That's what I'm trying to find out.'

'Look, when you guys got together, we did talk, we decided to never mention it, and we haven't. I never even think about it anymore.'

'Anymore? There you go. You wanted more, didn't you?'

'Calm down, Sherlock. Maybe I did, at the time. She's a top bird, Sam, you're a lucky man, but I'm over it. Got over it years ago.'

'It's all a bit weird.'

'It was one night, a long time ago.'

'Last weekend you refused to tell us who your best one-night stand was. You changed the subject, told us about that rub and tug you'd had in Singapore with some transvestite you fancied.'

'No Sam, she, sorry *he*, never pulled me off, it was an innocent massage, a misunderstanding. I was stiff, not *stiff*. Tired, I was tired. It was just a fucking massage. And I didn't fancy him, *her*.'

'Whatever, you were talking about Nicole, weren't you?'

'No.'

'Liar.'

'Okay, so what, I liked her, but it was only once. Besides, it was me who rang her up, got you two talking again, got her to meet you in the department store. It's not me she wants; she never wanted me. For some unknown reason she preferred you. You won, Sam. Satisfied now?'

'Not really.'

'Get over it.'

'Fuck off.'

'Very mature.'

I gulped hard on my pint and stared ahead. The unwritten laws of one-upmanship are the cornerstone of any male friendship. Donnie and I were no exception. And, for once, he was right. I had won. I think. It was suddenly all very complex. His father was a gangster, but he was somewhat indifferent to the ramifications of that. He sat very uncomfortably with the idea, with the history; whereas Connor and I thought it all very cool. He dated models but, as it turned out, envied my love life. He earned a mint. I helped young people. And what's more, I was starting to enjoy teaching again. Connor would no doubt now be in a position of management in the video store and, when all said and done, had been a gangster. When the dust settled, this would be a huge draw card, worth big points. Both Donnie and I had aided Connor's recovery and, in return, his mateship was our mutual asset. So I guess you could call it a draw.

So we did.

On nights like this I feel proud of our pub, the mood we'd created, the spirit of the place. No one ever mentioned it, but it was palpable. If a stranger walked in they'd no doubt sense its flipside, as if viewing crude negatives of what we all see and feel. But therein lies the point. It isn't special if just anyone can tap into it. It takes time; you have to earn the right. We did. And tonight we reaped our reward. Then, just as the party was flooring into top gear, the heartbeat of our pub stopped for a moment, our sense of community thrown into question. The spirit of The Fox and Hounds was about to be tested to its very perimeter.

At about nine-thirty a group of men walked in. To the majority they were strangers, yet they didn't go unnoticed. We knew who they were, the three of us; to us they were infamous, notorious, bad news all round. The atmosphere didn't overawe them, not in the slightest. Quite the contrary, they enjoyed gate-crashing our party, because they were hellbent on killing the atmosphere, and they were unlikely to stop there.

There were six of them. Again. They were tooled-up, carrying a variety of weaponry, including, on first glance: coshes, baseball bats, iron bars and metal chains. One of them, with the ponytail, carried a canister, presumably of petrol. They were clearly here to make a point, an example, a cultured disturbance.

It didn't take long for the rest of the pub to work out who they were.

And who they were after.

32
Monday: 9:33pm

It was the same six, led by Sharkhead who, unlike the apex predator he resembles, obviously couldn't survive long on the one kill. They were here for revenge, plain and simple. To save face. They were the same six who'd triggered the chain of events that led to tonight, to our celebration. And they were determined to complete the cycle their way. They were the O'Donnells' boys. One of them was responsible for sinking a knife into Techno Terry. My bet would be the one who stood at the front, baying, a film of sweat on his face, the saliva swilling in his mouth. Sharkhead. He obviously deemed insufficient the job done on Connor, leaving him to die, haemorrhaging warmth, on that unceremonious slab of wet concrete outside our home.

The pub fell silent upon their arrival. Large Barry turned the music off from behind the bar and everyone waited for something bad to happen. Sharkhead fixed his glare on me once again, my nose throbbing as he did so. He stood at the front of his mob, hands in his pockets, a familiar stance. Then he widened his glance and spoke to the pub as a whole.

242

'Word is it there's a cowardly little wanker in here that needs to be taught another lesson. He can't hide behind his bosses no more. He's been nothing but trouble and I'm personally going to take a lot of pleasure in doing to him what I did to his little pal in the warehouse. You lot have two choices - hand him over or get your pub trashed, then torched, with you inside it.'

At that moment he spotted Connor, over by the pool table. I was at the bar with Donnie, fresh from reconciliation.

He walked towards Connor.

And everyone else, including me, remained deadly still.

It hadn't crossed our minds that in releasing Connor from the hold of the Taylor boys he'd be left stranded; open slather to those he'd been protected from under the dubious wing of the Taylors. Somehow this lot knew the whole story; good news travels fast in a bad world. There was a moment of strained silence, broken only by his menacing footsteps. He stopped inches from Connor's face. Then his heavy hands left his pockets, grabbing Connor roughly by the throat. Connor gasped for air but did not flinch; instead staring back, hard. He was defiant, gaining strength from somewhere, from someone. He'd hardly recovered from the last bout. His face was still bruised, his ribs still cracked and his heart glued together. Now he faced more pain. Sharkhead pulled back his arm in readiness for what was sure to be a sickening blow. He looked so big in comparison to Connor, too big, dwarfing our friend, stealing his air.

Then I remembered something.

It's not about the size of the dog in the fight, but the size of the fight in the dog.

And just before the release of that thunderous punch there was a huge cry of 'no' from a section of the crowd. Someone ran to Connor's side, to his aid. And that person stood between the two men, his arm across Connor's chest, his eyes fixed on their enemy. And, almost in one movement, he threw a smart right fist into the jaw of the bully. The blow was a good one and knocked Sharkhead off balance, off his perch. He staggered, leaving just enough time for the two of them to retreat to the rabble.

It was me.

As hard as it is to believe, that person was me, Donnie by my side. We grabbed Connor, pulled him back. Suddenly onlookers turned into players, apathy into pride and locals into heroes; they moved and they spoke up. Some shouted, others cheered and before we knew it there was a crowd, shifting like one animal into the jaws and faces of Sharkhead and his mob. They stood, tall, firm, determined. Suddenly just about every adult male in the pub was standing, toe to toe, with the O'Donnells. Sharkhead rose, releasing an angry cry. Then he dived into our stubborn crowd. The fight was on.

There was a mass of flailing limbs, a wall of noise and colour. It lasted but seconds; an intensity of pressure that damn near tore the roof of the pub. Entering the fray first, unsurprisingly, was Misery Morris, a man well versed in the art of rucking. It was a busman's holiday to him, almost smiling as he fought. He grabbed Sharkhead in a headlock. Next was his good mate and pool rival, Darren 'Monkey' Taylor - the mechanic with the lucrative sideline in porn. He was yielding a wrench grabbed smartly from the toolbox he brought to the pub for fear it may get nicked from his car. Half the pub had the same idea, each helping themselves to a variety of implements and gizmos from the now half-empty box. Large Barry lifted the baseball bat he kept behind the bar and stood alongside his punters and friends. He'd never used it before, save for the odd late night game of pickled-egg softball. But he was ready to use it now. And use it he did, swinging wildly, catching the foreheads and backs of his opponents. Just the mere sniff of petrol, the threat of burning his life, had enraged our publican, building his nerve. Others, like Greek Tony, picked up pool cues and ashtrays, bottles and glasses, all weighing in for a piece of folklore. This was personal, for all of us.

A couple of swift blows from Misery, a speculative wield from Large and a sneaky ashtray to the gob from Tony and it was pretty much all over. Again, Donnie managed a couple of well-placed jabs and I'm sure, amongst the blur and heave of muscle and noise, I witnessed Connor laying several boots into a stricken Sharkhead. They, like us before them, were outnumbered, left no option but to down arms, raise hands and remain on the floor, surrounded by dirt, dust and spilt alcohol. They were shaken by our collective counter; shamed by their own downfall.

In truth it wasn't just the groundswell of public intent that had elicited their premature trouncing. They'd seen something else. Moreover, they'd seen *someone* else, and they'd seen enough. For, standing at the back of the pub, behind me and behind the throng of locals, were two more men; two ordinary looking blokes, both past their physical peak, neither one armed, but both spelling some sort of danger for anyone who crossed them.

Bob Rossi and Danny Taylor.

They were faces. They were known. Ghosts of the past, the pair of them. This was especially true of Danny. So what had begun as a spot of timely revenge on a bit-part player had suddenly turned into a potentially gruesome brawl with an infamous operator from days gone by, with all the after sales service of an old school campaigner. It was too much to manage. And if these guys knew the history of their chosen profession they'd have realised that the guy standing beside him was there at the beginning, at grass roots level, when it wasn't about drugs, when it was about existence, of knowing when to thrive and when to survive - a lesson I had only recently learned myself.

When the O'Donnell boys clocked the magnitude of the job, it was suddenly deemed counter-productive, and thrown into the basket marked *not worth it*. I knew we wouldn't be seeing them again. And I was proud of our pub, our efforts. We'd stood our ground and we'd made our point. Bob and Danny said nothing to them. They didn't have to. Bob simply threw me another wink, patted me on the back and ordered me a lager.

'Gorgeous right hand, that, Sam,' he croaked, puffing hard on a victorious cigar, professional, paternal. 'You cleaned the bloke up. And I see my boy Donnie's got a solid shot, too. Chip off the old block, eh. Don't tell him I said so though. He don't like me enjoying a scrap, banging on about the old days. Fair enough, I suppose. Violence ain't no answer.'

'Can't half be fun though, Bob.'

'You're not fucking wrong there, Sammy-boy.'

And we laughed. And I was sure that we'd all be harping on about that particular scrap for some time to come.

Then I thought of how Donnie had tried to reason with those people, how it had all started. He'd managed to soften up one gangster, namely his father, so I guess he thought he could do the same with these guys. But it's different with family and friends. And I figured it really wasn't worth dwelling on him and Nicole. The future was too good-looking. Even better looking than Donnie. And our friendship, my relationship, they were way more important right now. The O'Donnell boys hadn't bargained on coming up against that sort of solidarity, mainly because we hadn't bargained on producing it. We didn't really know it existed until the backbone of the pub and its punters were questioned. And as the O'Donnells left, so the Fox and Hounds witnessed the loudest cheer of the night. I suspect it was the loudest cheer in its history. And the biggest grin belonged to Connor. He felt more empowered at that moment than at any time working as a gangster.

The arrival of Kathy and Amber prompted the first account of the night's events. And so the myth was born. We recounted the legendary performances of the locals. But their arrival also triggered concern. Nicole had yet to return from her phone call. Now we'd offloaded the O'Donnell crew onto the street outside, licking their wounds, smarting from their loss. They could be anywhere, so could Nicole. The fear rose inside me, bubbling. I reached into my pocket for my mobile. It began to ring, then cut off. Now I was really scared. I leapt up, ran for the door. But it swung open wildly before I could grab the handle, throwing me to the ground in a heap.

Then Nicole walked through. And she wasn't alone. She had another man with her, on her arm.

My father.

He walked in, looked down, smiled and offered me his hand. He pulled me up, dusted me down, then complemented me on my jacket.

We ordered a drink, sat down and talked. The three of us. Nothing too heavy. Again, there was plenty of time for that. And it was good to see him. It was good to hear him talk, to listen to him tell me how proud he was, of the engagement, of my work with Rory, how he'd missed me.

And how he was sorry.

I told them the story of the night. They needed to know, they were locals too. And it was an important night; a night that would go down in the folklore of The Fox and Hounds, in our heads and hearts.

It would be the night we stemmed the flow of bad blood, for good.

Printed in the United Kingdom
by Lightning Source UK Ltd.
119242UK00001B/25